ZOeY DeaN's
STar POWer

ZOEY DEAN'S
STAR POWER

A TALENT NOVEL

razor
bill

Starpower

RAZORBILL

Published by the Penguin Group
Penguin Young Readers Group
345 Hudson Street, New York, New York 10014, U.S.A
Penguin Group (USA) Inc., 375 Hudson Street, New York, New York 10014, U.S.A
Penguin Group (Canada), 90 Eglinton Avenue East, Suite 700, Toronto, Ontario,
Canada M4P 2Y3 (a division of Pearson Penguin Canada Inc.)
Penguin Books Ltd, 80 Strand, London WC2R 0RL, England
Penguin Ireland, 25 St Stephen's Green, Dublin 2, Ireland
(a division of Penguin Books Ltd)
Penguin Group (Australia), 250 Camberwell Road, Camberwell, Victoria 3124,
Australia (a division of Pearson Australia Group Pty Ltd)
Penguin Books India Pvt Ltd, 11 Community Centre, Panchsheel Park,
New Delhi–110 017, India
Penguin Group (NZ), Cnr Airborne and Rosedale Roads, Albany, Auckland 1310,
New Zealand (a division of Pearson New Zealand Ltd)
Penguin Books (South Africa) (Pty) Ltd, 24 Sturdee Avenue, Rosebank,
Johannesburg 2196, South Africa

Penguin Books Ltd, Registered Offices: 80 Strand, London WC2R 0RL, England

10 9 8 7 6 5 4 3 2 1

alloyentertainment

Produced by Alloy Entertainment
151 West 26th Street
New York, NY 10001

Library of Congress Cataloging-in-Publication data is available

Printed in the United States of America

For Alyse and George

zoey dean's
star power

CHAPTER ONE

emily

◄ **Wednesday**   September 23 ►

12:45 PM	Check out of school
1 PM	Power lunch at Ford's Filling Station
2 PM	Arrive at Sony lot
2:30 PM	Meet with director

"Okay, my future star, we're almost done!" Mackenzie Little-Armstrong whipped around from the front seat of the silver Prius to face Emily Mungler. "Just a few more Hollywood rules."

Emily nervously twirled her cinnamon brown hair around her index finger. She was scrunched in the back seat between her two other best friends in Los Angeles, Cordelia Kingsley (aka Coco) and Evangelina Becks (aka Becks), on the way to rehearsals for her new movie, *Deal With It*. Mac was teaching her the cardinal rules of making it in Tinseltown, which were turning out to be more complicated than Lindsay Lohan's love life.

"Okay. Last one: Hollywood is very clique-y. It's like BAMS," she added, referring to their junior high, Bel-Air Middle School, "but with waaaaay more ego."

"So true." Mac's assistant, Erin, who was driving them across town, nodded in agreement. Erin was twenty-seven, and she had green eyes and extraordi-

2

narily pale skin. Technically, Erin worked as one of four assistants to Mac's mother, Adrienne Little-Armstrong, the most powerful agent in Hollywood. But the reality was that Erin spent most of her days schlepping around Mac and her entourage.

"Let's review one more time," Mac said, twisting her waist-length blond hair into a knot. "What does everyone love?" she quizzed.

"Confidence," Emily shot back. "Even if I have to fake it."

"Great." Mac looked down at her iPhone and read from her notes. "What's the rule about hanging out with extras?"

"I can't be too friendly, or my star power will go down." Emily winced. Mac's rules were a tad snobby.

"Perfection!" Mac cooed. "When can you gossip?"

"Never?" Emily asked, even though she hadn't meant it as a question.

"Trick question." Mac tilted the rearview mirror to make eye contact with Emily. "Never gossip *unless* you need information. Then you give a little to get a little. You just have to be *strategic*."

Emily's heartbeat quickened. She was an actress, not a spy. Besides, nothing she'd done here in Hollywood had been strategic. It had all happened by accident a month ago, when Mac discovered Emily at a premiere party. Back then she was just Emily Mungler, from Cedartown, Iowa. Now she was Emily *Skylar*—Mac, her

3

agent and best friend, had assigned her a catchier stage name—and she lived with Mac in Bel-Air, one of the ritziest neighborhoods in the world.

"Just remember." Mac turned to face her, her lightly freckled face stern and her light blue eyes serious. "When you step on set, you're entering a no-trust zone. Kimmie Tachman is live-blogging her experience as an assistant 'producer.'" Mac made air quotes around the word *producer* because everyone knew that Kimmie's dad, who was actually producing *Deal With It*, had just given her the title so she'd see her name at the end of the credits. "Just because she goes to BAMS with us does not mean she's safe. In fact, quite the opposite."

Emily nodded and thought about how her mom, Lori, would tell her to "just enjoy the now." Her mother was always reading self-help books, by everyone from Deepak Chopra to that guy Oprah loved with the weird name. Emily tried to "enjoy the now" while she stared out at the palm trees. She hadn't even realized her leg was twitching until Coco put a hand on her knee.

Mac started again. "Oh, also—"

"Snap, Mac!" Coco cut her off. "Do you need a Yoga Power Hour? You're scaring Em!" Coco was always the first to rush to someone's defense when Mac got too bossy, which was why Emily loved her.

"You're freaking *me* out," Becks said. She looked like a model but only cared about two things: surfing and her friends.

4

"We're almost done," Mac insisted. She removed an invisible fleck of dust from her navy Ella Moss Collection dress. "Last but not least: Who is always, always, always right?"

"The director," Emily said quickly. That, at least, was a no-brainer.

"Congrats, babe. You're almost in." Mac flashed a devilish grin. "You'll know you're *really* in Hollywood when you're stabbing someone in the back or you're getting stabbed in the back."

Just then, Mac's phone blared its Fergilicious ringtone.

"Talk to me!" she barked. Everyone in the car was quiet—you never knew who was going to call Mac. She shook her head impatiently. "N-n-no, this is *Mac*. . . . Yes, Davey."

It was Davey Farris Woodward, aka Emily's costar, aka her lifelong crush and the reason she'd come to L.A. in the first place! Coco and Becks playfully nudged Emily in the ribs, knowing how much she liked him. Except she didn't just *like* him—she'd literally plastered her bedroom walls back in Iowa with his photos, ripped from *Star*, *People*, and *Us Weekly*. All Emily wanted in life was to a) act and b) make Davey Farris Woodward fall in love with her (and not necessarily in that order). Which was why she craned her neck to hear every second of Mac's conversation.

"My mom's at work," Mac continued in her usual no-

nonsense tone. Davey was Adrienne Little-Armstrong's biggest client. "Have you tried her office? . . . No, this is *my* cell phone. . . . Yep, that's the number. . . . Noproblemokaybyeeee."

"Davey Woodward is a moron!" Mac announced as she ended the call. "He forgets everything!"

"Well, *you* forgot to tell him to fall in love with Emily on set!" Becks blurted. Coco, Mac, and Becks giggled appreciatively.

For the next two weeks of the shoot, Emily would have to look, dress, and act like a guy, opposite the only guy she had ever hearted. *Deal With It* was about a girl who disguised herself as a boy in order to attend an all-boys' prep school and play on the soccer team. Cute in theory, but not cute when the FLOHL (Future Love of Her Life) was going to see her in baggy shorts all day. Emily had made a new rule to look exceptionally cute when she arrived on set so that Davey could see her as his PG (Potential Girlfriend). Then they could fall in love and go for romantic hikes in Runyon Canyon with one of Davey's adopted mutt mixes, who would scamper onto rocks and bark at butterflies while she and Davey walked hand in hand, pausing occasionally to look at the clear California view and share their very first offscreen kiss with the Hollywood sign in the background. . . .

Emily was so busy fantasizing about her future love life that she didn't realize the car had pulled up in front of the giant iron gates to the Sony lot. Emily gulped. It was like being the new girl on the first day of school all over again—except that this was the coolest school in the world.

"Break a leg!" Mac chimed as she turned around and waved at Emily.

And then Emily realized: Mac was waving *goodbye.* As in: Mac wasn't going with her. "Aren't you coming with me?"

"Negative," Mac said, slipping on her new Dita sunglasses. She gestured toward Coco and Becks, who had begun playing Guitar Hero on Tour on their DS. "We've got work to do."

Coco blew one air kiss and Becks waved as Emily crawled out of the car. She shut the door dejectedly and watched the Prius drive away. Her heart began racing, the back of her neck went cold, and her leg started trembling so much it was hard to walk. Emily wondered if every day of her new life was going to be this nervewracking. And if so, was it worth it?

Before she could answer her own question, she felt a tap on her shoulder. "Miss Skylar?"

Emily spun on her baby blue Havaianas, wondering who in the world would be calling her "Miss." She turned to face the tallest, skinniest boy she had ever seen. He looked about sixteen. Emily was pretty sure that he was a production assistant, because he was wearing a headset and holding a clipboard.

"I'm Chris Miller," the boy said, extending a thin forearm. He wore baggy taupe corduroys, orange and yellow Pumas with green laces, and a faded black T-shirt that said FRANCIS FORD COPPOLA'S THE GODFATHER. His hazel eyes were the same shade as his hair, which flopped onto his long golden eyelashes. His right eyebrow was pierced with a tiny nail.

"You can call me Chris," he continued. "Or you can be like all the other egomaniacs and snap your fingers in front of my face."

"Hmm . . ." Emily pretended to think about it. "I think I'll go with Chris."

"Cool." Chris nodded. "You'll be the first person all summer to know my name."

Emily laughed and Chris smiled like he was handing out a VIP pass into his good graces. "I'll show you to your trailer," he said, adjusting his headset. "Follow me."

They walked through the Sony lot, passing the other soundstages. It was like being at Epcot Center: Every soundstange was a mini universe built to look exactly like ancient Rome, or Mars, or New York City. And Emily kept noticing familiar people. In front of Soundstage No. 5, Selena Gomez was talking to a man in a business suit, while Emmy Rossum entered, clutching a coffee drink. In front of Soundstage No. 11, La Lohan herself walked by holding what appeared to be a . . . chinchilla. No wonder it was so hard to spot stars in L.A.—they were all here! Emily tried to remember everything so that she could give Paige a full report.

Emily smile-nodded. "I feel like I'm officially in Hollywood."

"Easy, tiger," Chris said, leading her to a set of double doors marked SOUNDSTAGE NO. 13: SCHOOL. "You know what they say—you're not in Hollywood unless someone's stab–"

"Oh no!" Emily pretended to cover her ears with her hands. "I've heard it already. It can't be true."

"I feel ya," Chris said thoughtfully. "But it's true." With that, he flung open the doors to Soundstage No. 13. It was like that moment in the *Wizard of Oz* when everything went into Technicolor, but instead, Emily's world magically morphed into New England. There were various sets designed to look like boarding school interiors—one stage was a library, another was an oak-paneled classroom, and another held a dining hall with a giant table and stained glass windows.

Chris led Emily through the soundstages and then out the other side to a giant parking lot. Finally they arrived at a white trailer. Chris tapped the giant gold star on the front that said EMILY SKYLAR. "Home sweet home."

Emily took dainty steps up the metal staircase to peer inside. The first thing she saw was a circular mirror dotted with big lightbulbs. Next to that was a kitchenette with a giant platter of chocolate chip cookies on the counter. A table by the couch was covered in gift bags from Marni, Gucci, Anthropologie, and Ron Herman. "What's all this?" Emily asked.

"They're start gifts for you." Chris shrugged. "I sign for them every day. You got one from Adrienne Little-Armstrong, from the director, from your on-set tutor, the casting director, Davey Woodward. . . ."

Davey had gotten her a present? Emily's heart soared.

"And I'm sure they all picked them out themselves. . . ."

"Really?" Emily asked, touched.

"No!" Chris scoffed. "That's what assistants are for."

"Oh," Emily's heart sank a little, knowing that Davey hadn't actually chosen her gift himself, but she tried to hide her disappointment. The last thing she wanted was for everyone to find out that she had a major crush on her costar.

Spotting the large closet marked WARDROBE, Emily walked over and cautiously opened the doors. She braced herself for flannel and other embarrassingly hideous boy costumes.

But as she peered inside the closet, she didn't see gross boy-jeans or boy-shirts or anything boy at all. Instead she saw a colorful assortment of Alice + Olivia dresses and Milly blouses and cute Rock & Republics. Tags from Nanette Lepore, Tibi, and Rachel Pally poked out. Even the closet floor was dotted with velvety shoe bags from Christian Louboutin and Loeffler Randall.

"Um . . . Chris?" Emily said meekly. "I think there's been a mistake."

Chris rushed over. "Did we get you the wrong sizes?"

"No, that's not it at all. It's just that these are all *girl* clothes," she said. *The most awesome girl clothes in the world,* she mentally added. "And I don't ever get to be a girl in the movie."

"Uh . . ." Chris stammered. He looked terrified.

"Maybe I'm in the wrong trailer?" Emily suggested.

Just then a voice boomed, *"Change in plans, Doll-face!"*

Emily turned around and faced her director, Shane Reed. He wore an all-white suit with his signature cream fedora, and was flanked by his assistant, Giselle, a tall supermodel-like creature who had been at Emily's audition. Giselle almost never spoke or showed emotion. She smiled coolly.

Emily felt dizzy: Of course there had been a change in plans. They'd probably fired her and replaced her with a real actress. Someone who had actually been in movies. Emily put her hand on the closet door to steady herself.

Shane put his hands on his hips and studied Emily like she was the last square in a sudoku puzzle. "Look how cute and nervous she looks!" he commented to no one in particular. "What are you worried about? Don't worry, we're not replacing *you*."

Emily smiled with relief.

Shane scratched his neck. "We're replacing the *script*. Apparently this movie has already been made. It's called *She's the Man*. And *apparently* no one thought to tell me that when I agreed to direct this bad boy." He shot a glare at Giselle. "So I guess He's the Fool." He pointed at himself.

Emily nodded once to show she understood, but did not think Shane was the fool.

"You *did* get the revised script?" Shane asked. Emily wasn't sure if Shane was talking to her or Giselle.

Emily shook her head, and Giselle began muttering something about "new script to Emily."

"Does anyone work around here?" Shane looked at Chris and snapped his fingers. "I need a water."

Chris nodded obediently, went to the refrigerator, and wordlessly handed Shane a Metromint water.

"So we made a few tweaks to the plot," Shane said. Emily crossed her fingers, hoping the tweaks hadn't affected her twenty-eight scenes with Davey or her 914 lines of dialogue.

Shane took a giant swig of the Metromint water and chucked it into the recycling bin. "So here's the pitch: Davey's a computer nerd from the wrong side of the tracks. All he wants is to study computers and rule Google. Problem is, the best facility in America is at a girls' school that just got an awesome grant. So *he* pretends to be a girl named Tiffany so he can follow his dream. And then he meets your character, Kelly, and you both fall in love over a keyboard, hijinks ensue, yada yada yada . . ."

"Everything Davey was doing—now *you're* doing. And it's great, 'cause no one's *ever* seen a guy trying to be a girl. Except *Tootsie* or *Mrs. Doubtfire*, but those were a thousand years ago, without hotties like Davey."

Emily's heartbeat slowed to a normal pace. So she would still get her scenes with Davey, and. . . . "You mean, I'm going to be a girl *the whole time*?"

"Bingo, Buttercup!"

Emily suddenly felt like she was floating. It was like she'd already gotten the happy ending to her fairy-tale life. She had great friends in Los Angeles, a starring role in next summer's blockbuster, and now, thanks to Shane's change in plans, not only was she going to see her crush every single day, but she was going to actually *look like a girl* when she saw him, with her hair and makeup done by the best stylists in Hollywood. Now all she needed was a kiss from her prince charming and her story would be complete.

Emily looked at her reflection in the brightly lit vanity mirror and smiled. A romance with Davey seemed as inevitable as another Britney breakdown—all she had to do was wait.

chapter
TWO

◄ Wednesday   September 23 ►

4 PM   Coco discovers her destiny!!!

Reminder: TAKE CHARGE!

Mac flipped on her aviators and smiled as the car cruised past the Pacific Design Center, one of her favorite buildings in L.A. Her girls were on track for the next phase of MHD (Mission: Hollywood Domination).

She reached into the canvas shopping bag at her feet and pulled out some kombucha for her friends. She put one in the cup holder for Erin, who was driving.

"Cheers to us!" Mac lifted her sparkling tea. "Red carpets, here we come!"

"Cheers!" Becks and Coco cried in unison.

Mac smiled as she sipped her fizzy drink triumphantly and felt the warm wind from outside whip through her hair. Earlier that month, they had been the laughingstock of BAMS after their classmate Ruby Goldman leaked a video of their slumber party to the entire school. Mac shivered just thinking about how everyone had seen the clip of her gas leakage incident, of Coco basically wetting her pants, of Emily making fun of Kimmie, and of Becks practicing her kissing skills on a frozen yogurt. And yet, Mac thought proudly, it was amazing how quickly you could make a comeback if you were smart about it. Now Mac was hanging out with movie stars and missing school while Ruby was still going to BAMS with the rest of the plebes in town.

Mac turned around to the backseat. "You guys *have* to keep me posted on Ruby while I'm out of school, 'kay?" Mac had worked out a deal with her mother that she could skip school and work on the movie (and have on-set tutoring) as long as she maintained her good grades, kept up her family obligations, and wrote up a report about the value of the experience. She'd even signed it with her little sister, Maude, as a witness. "I need you girls to be my eyes and ears at BAMS. I want to know everything."

"I'll live-blog for you," Coco joked, and then glanced down at her iPhone. "I see we are going to Discover My Destiny." The girls had synched their calendars so that they could all keep track of each other's schedules. (Or really, so Mac could keep track of them.) Earlier that week, Mac had realized that Coco's destiny was to be a folksy alterna-singer like Colby Caillat (but more indie!). What Mac hadn't told her yet was *how* they were going to go about it.

"That's correct," Mac said mysteriously. She knew

Coco was waiting for her to go on, but she preferred keeping her in suspense. Mac had decided it wasn't necessary to get into the details with her friends. Years of studying her mother, who was, after all, the most powerful agent in Hollywood, had shown Mac that A-list managers took control, made decisions, and led their clients—sometimes forcibly—down the necessary path. Left on their own, Mac's friends might happily read *Us Weekly* instead of being in *Us Weekly*. Without her, they'd never reach their full potential. Which was why Mac had set up a daily iPhone reminder with her new mantra: *Take charge*.

"As long as Coco's destiny is not in a mall, I'm fine," Becks offered as they passed the Beverly Center. She liked shopping as much as Mac liked back fat.

"I know where we're going, but I won't say," Erin singsonged from the driver's seat. Mac shot a *don't you dare* look at Erin, who smiled proudly, loving that she was in on Mac's secret. Sometimes Mac appreciated having Erin in her fan club. Other times (like now) it made her sad that Erin was twenty-seven and still a follower. Why didn't she just become a lawyer, or do something with her Princeton degree? Mac shuddered, stuffing the idea away like a muffin-top in skinny jeans. She couldn't manage *everyone's* life.

As the Prius cruised eastward, no one said anything for miles. They silently sailed farther from the ocean, cruising over the Hollywood Hills overlooking the downtown L.A. skyline. Soon the air became thicker and grayer. Even the palm trees looked exhausted.

"We're really far *east*," Coco said finally, when they passed a run-down freeway ramp. She said "east" like she was looking at a tabloid picture of Kim Kardashian. The only time they ventured east of La Brea was to go to VIP parties at Teddy's—but that was at night. "I've never been this way in the afternoon. . . ." Coco finished, fishing for clues. Mac kept a Mona Lisa smile on her face.

Finally they reached the wasteland better known as Hollywood Boulevard. Despite its glamorous name, the street was just a tourist trap with gold stars on the sidewalk. Mac kept a perfect poker face as Erin turned onto a narrow street and pulled the car into a dinky strip mall, where a dilapidated sign said KARMA CAFÉ in hand-painted wobbly letters. It appeared to have been drawn by a three-year-old.

"Voilà!" Mac proclaimed proudly, as though she had surprised the girls with a trip to Paris.

Coco and Becks exchanged a nervous glance.

Mac tossed an air kiss at Coco. "Ciao bella! Have fun!" She pointed at Becks. "We need to hit the beach."

"Are you for serious?" Coco stayed planted in the car, clutching her seat belt. "I'm not going in there."

Mac had expected this. "You have to. How else can you check out your competition?"

"My *what*?" Coco made a face as though Mac had forced her to wear pink Uggs.

Mac smiled sweetly. "Anyone in there is competing with you on the coffee shop circuit for fans."

"Um, Mac?" Coco reminded her friend. "I'm not on the coffee shop circuit."

"Not *yet*," Mac corrected. "But if you're going to be the next Colby Caillat but more indie, then you're going to have to sing in indie places—ergo coffee houses—and build your fan base from the ground up."

Coco grimaced. "What's wrong with Urth Café?" Urth was the quintessential L.A. café where power agents and stars sipped no-fat, half-caf, no-sugar-added lattes. However, Mac had learned from her early research that Karma Café was the quintessential low-budget, independent, anti-Starbucks venue where Coco could start getting indie street cred. It had nightly gigs and a regular audience of alterna-kids.

"Nothing's wrong with Urth," Mac said. "Except that we like it, and my mom likes it, and the rest of Hollywood likes it, ergo"—she was really loving the word *ergo* these days—"you can't begin an indie career there." She twirled her Mintee bracelet on her tan wrist. "Work with me, Co. Erin will be back to pick you up. For now, watch and learn."

"But—"

Mac shook her head and Coco begrudgingly got out of the car, her Tory Burch ankle boots tapping on the asphalt.

As the car pulled away, Mac cringed, seeing Coco's sad, stooped posture. She closed her eyes and reminded herself that sometimes being a good friend meant leaving your bestie with people who didn't wear deodorant, if that would help her reach her dreams.

Mac sighed. Sometimes true love was tough love.

CHAPTER THREE

becks

◀ Wednesday   September 23 ▶

6 PM   Destiny Meeting at Dixie Surf Company
        Corporate Headquarters

8:30 PM Evening yoga with Deepti on back patio

B ecks and Mac sat on ocean blue sofas in the waiting room of the Dixie Surf Company Corporate
Headquarters. Becks tried to stay chill, but her
eyes bounced around the room, checking out the giant
posters of Laird Hamilton, Kelly Slater, and Alessa
Quizon.

If Mac was for real, Becks was one meeting away
from becoming the fourth Dixie Gal. They were a team
of three surfers (Tully, Darby, and Leilani) who were
flown to exotic beaches in places like the Maldives and
competed in international surfing competitions so they
could be photographed in Dixie surf gear. Their pictures
wound up in Dixie stores, surf magazines, and surf calendars. In fact, Becks had a Dixie Gals calendar on the
back of her bedroom door. "Remind me again how you
got this meeting?"

"I have my ways," Mac said flippantly as she
checked the five-day weather forecast on her iPhone.

Of course it was the same every day: eighty degrees and sunny.

"But how do you know I'm even ready?" Becks asked. Sure, Mac knew a lot about movie stars, but the surfing world was another universe. And Becks had figured that she needed at least another three years before she'd be good enough to turn pro and represent a brand.

"I did some research." Mac looked at her friend. "Actually, I did a *lot* of research."

Just then a man with tanned skin and bright blond hair emerged from behind a white door, his flip-flops smacking the shiny marble floor. Becks blushed when she recognized Chad Hutchins. The last time she'd seen him had been at the Quiksilver store at the Grove, when she had been forced to take Ellie, a girl from their grade in BAMS, shopping for surfing gear. He had thought that Ellie was the surfer, not Becks, and she was embarrassed just thinking about how she had tried (and failed) to explain that she was actually a really good surfer. She hoped he'd forgotten the incident.

"Buddy! It's you!" Chad exclaimed, recognizing her instantly. "Forgot your name!"

"Evangelina Becks." Mac stood automatically.

Chad was still looking at Becks, like he was trying to remember how they knew each other. Then he snapped his fingers. "Yeah . . . met you at the Grove. . . . So I work for Dixie now. . . . Small world, huh?" He clapped his hands together.

Becks removed her right hand from the pocket of her hoodie and waved shyly at Chad. She instantly regretted the move. She should have said *something* to him—it was weird to wave when someone was talking to you. Why did she go mute every time she got nervous?

"I'm Mackenzie Little-Armstrong," Mac said, firmly shaking Chad's hand.

Chad sized up Mac, shaking his head. "Wow, you really are thirteen." He chuckled. "I've never met an agent your age."

"And you never will again." Mac smiled. "So, where are we meeting?"

"Right this way. Come meet my team." He held the door open and Becks peered inside a conference room that was big enough to host twenty people. In the middle was a giant blue table with rippled edges like a wave. Floor-to-ceiling glass walls revealed an unobstructed view of the Santa Monica Pier, where the sun was shimmering over the roller coaster. On the side wall were three clocks; each one told the time in a different surfing destination: Huntington, Pipeline, and Bondi.

Two people sat at the table. A woman with bleached blond hair and freckles was at the head. She wore a red sleeveless Patagonia fleece, exposing her chiseled arm muscles. Her face was very tanned except for the pale circles around her eyes where sunglasses apparently went. A few seats away from her sat a guy in a Billabong

T-shirt who looked about thirty. His brown hair was so curly that it looked like a clown wig.

They were both eating submarine sandwiches and crunching on potato chips, which explained why the room smelled like barbecue sauce. They shot confused glances at Chad, like they had not been expecting this meeting.

Chad put his fingers in his mouth and whistled. "Listen up, peeps!" He pointed at Mac with his thumb, like he was hitchhiking. "I got here Mackenzie Little-A." Then Chad studied Becks, his face scrunched in confusion. He lowered his voice to a stage whisper. "Buddy, sorry. I keep forgettin' your name."

"Everyone calls her Becks. One word," Mac reminded him. "Like Rihanna."

The executives laughed. Becks wasn't sure if they were laughing at Mac or if the moment had been funny in some way that she didn't register. She tried to make eye contact with Mac, but Mac was still smiling at full attention.

"Okay, Mac and Becks," Chad said, "I'd like you to meet our head of advertising, Dale Goody." He pointed to Crazy Curls, who was reaching into his mouth to pick at his teeth, "and the founder of our company, Liz Dixie." Chad took a seat between them.

Becks wanted to say goodbye and leave them to their lunch, but to her horror Mac eased confidently into an empty swivel chair across from the executives and patted the seat next to her, motioning for Becks to follow. Becks started to get that feeling she sometimes got when she was surfing—like she'd picked the wrong wave and a wipeout was inevitable. Except that she hadn't picked this wave.

"Thank you so much—" Mac began.

"Listen, Mackie," Chad cut her off. "Here's the deal." He drummed his fingers on the table. "I originally took this meeting so you'd stop hounding me."

Beck's stomach churned. Of course it had been too good to be true. She looked for the door and wondered if it would be crazy to run out *rightthissecond*.

"But your timing is actually really right on," Chad continued, "because our fourth Dixie Gal didn't, ahem, quite work out. So we're actually holding tryouts for a new fourth this weekend." He looked at Becks. "How old are you?"

The way he phrased the question, Becks was sure there was a wrong answer. She pursed her lips and tried to think of different answers to the question. She could only think of one. "Thirteen?" she finally squeaked.

"Yeah, I was afraid of that. Our minimum cut-off age is usually fifteen." Chad looked genuinely disappointed. "Too bad, 'cause I checked out the clips of you on YouTube that Mac e-mailed. You're pretty hard-core."

Becks blushed. She had no idea Mac had been sending her homemade surfing videos to strangers.

Mac seized the opportunity. "Going young would

26

be the smart thing to do, since she can grow with the brand. Plus, Becks is tall enough to look fifteen, and she can totally hang with the Dixie Gals. And this is coming from the demographic you're trying to sell—"

Chad opened his mouth to speak, but Liz put her hand out to silence him. "Let her finish," she said firmly.

Mac clasped her hands. "Here's the thing. Yes, you guys are leading national sales of athletic bikini brands, but you could do even better. Especially in SoCal," Mac said. "Fortunately, I was able to get my family's accountant to crunch some numbers for you." She whipped out a pile of glossy pages from a clear plastic folder and handed one each to Liz, Chad, and Dale. "You're lagging in sales in your own state because people here go for brands endorsed by real surfers. The problem is that you're picking models over talent. Tully, Darby, and Leilani—no one doubts they can surf, but what you need is the Michael Phelps of girls' surfing." Then she looked at Becks adoringly. "And here she is."

Liz nodded slowly. "Funny you bring this up," she said, looking at the men. "We just had a meeting about this."

Becks could feel the eyes in the room landing on her like flies on half-eaten fruit. She hated being the center of attention. The only person not looking at her was Chad—he was staring at the glossy one-page Mac had just distributed, which was titled "Next Wave for Dixie:

Evangelina Becks." Becks cringed, spotting the giant picture of herself in the middle.

Mac sailed ahead. "Um, question," she began, reading notes off her iPhone. "Do any of your girls have the full backing of world champion Kelly Slater?"

The executives shook their heads.

Mac continued reading from her screen. "How many of your girls surfed Pipeline . . . before their fourteenth birthday? I'm guessing none?"

The executives again shook their heads.

Becks stared at her childhood best friend in awe. She noticed that all the executives were looking at Mac just as wide-eyed as she was. Liz Dixie was actually *taking notes* on things Mac said.

Mac still wasn't done. "Obviously Becks is adorable, but more importantly, she's the next colossal thing in your sport. So if I were you, I'd want to sign her today before someone else does." Mac gave them a sympathetic look. "Or you'll be knocked out of the SoCal market for good."

To Becks's surprise, there was silence. No chip chomping. No dental hygiene. Only the ticking of the three clocks.

Liz cleared her throat and looked at Becks. "Obviously, you're a beautiful girl," she said. Becks grimaced. *Here it comes*, she thought, knowing there would be a "but." *Here comes rejection*.

"YesIgetitthanksforeverything," Becks blurted. She

stood up and turned toward the door, but in her haste, Becks knocked over her chair. It crashed to the ground, making a loud *thud*. Then, reaching to pick it up, she knocked over Dale's drink, sending peach-colored Jamba Juice all over the blue table. Becks glanced frantically around the room for napkins. Seeing none, she yanked off her sweatshirt and began mopping the table with it. Suddenly she had gone from quiet surfer girl to clumsy freak show. She blushed so brightly that her cheeks hurt.

"She's much better in the water than on land," Mac offered.

The room laughed.

"As I was saying," Liz cleared her throat. "We *might* have an opening for a new fourth Dixie Gal, and we'd be willing to reconsider the age restrictions, but we have to see you on a board and see how you fit in with the group." Liz smiled. "The one thing we've learned is that the group dynamic is key."

Becks froze, her palm in a puddle of yogurty slop, a shy grin spreading across her face. Did that mean she had a chance after all? Her heart pounded and suddenly she didn't mind that her hands were sticky with smoothie or that her favorite sweatshirt was now an overpriced sponge.

"There are a lot of good-looking girls who think they can surf." Chad shook his head like it was a great travesty. "But most of them are useless on a board."

"Come to the tryouts in Manhattan Beach this weekend," Liz offered kindly. "If nothing else, it will be some good surfing."

Dale had finished his sandwich and was wiping his fingers one by one with a paper napkin. He nodded approvingly, his clown curls bobbing.

"Greatthanksthatsoundsreallyreallygreat!" Becks said, trying not to freak out.

"We appreciate this opportunity," Mac said, sounding professional. She leaned down and calmly reset the overturned chair and pushed Becks's smoothie-sopped sweatshirt into her Prada bowling bag with a *slop*. She smiled. "Thank you so much. The best is yet to come."

Still burning with embarrassment, Becks followed Mac out to the parking lot. Erin was waiting in the Prius, crunching on dried wasabi peas. Mac and Becks climbed into the car, slammed the doors shut, and didn't say a word. They waited until Erin had started the car and turned onto Abbot-Kinney Boulevard, safely out of Dixie territory, and then, in unison, they shrieked.

"Ahhhhhhhhh!"

"Ahhhhhhhhh!"

"Becks, they're gonna love you!" Mac exclaimed.

"I know!" Becks cried. Then she covered her mouth, embarrassed she had sounded so conceited. But the only thing about herself that Becks believed in 100 percent was her ability on a board.

"Wa-hoo!" Mac flashed the hang-loose sign, with her thumb and pinky sticking out. "Cowabunga, brah!"

Becks winced. "Mac, you know that's totally poser, right?"

Mac grinned broadly. "But you'll have to admit I was pretty, ahem, *tubular* in that meeting!"

Becks groaned. "We have to work on your slang."

"Kidding, B! You know I don't speak surfing." Mac stuck her hand behind her head to flash Becks the hang-loose sign yet again. "But I speak Hollywood, bébé, and we are riding one awesome wave."

Then she cranked up KIIS FM and they giggled all the way back to Malibu.

chapter
Four

COCO

◀ Friday   September 25 ▶

7 AM   Morning Rooftop Yoga

6 PM   Begin Karma Café disaster

9:15 PM   Sugar scrub in spa to get Karma Café's "karma" off me

Coco could not believe that she was a) *back* at Karma Café and b) next up to perform. On Wednesday she'd watched a few sad acts, and was ready to bail when Mac sent her a text ordering her to sign up to perform Friday night. Now she was sitting with the Inner Circle on an orange couch, sipping an organic, fair-trade mocha. Erin sat across from them in a green wooden chair, reading a *Spin* magazine that was two years old and tattered.

Everything about Karma Café was old and tattered: There was a bulletin board covered with a mess of thumbtacks and so many yellowed papers on top of each other that all of the notices were unreadable. The tables and chairs were mismatched and/or missing legs. Even the people looked out of whack, like they were still waiting for their chai to kick in.

In the center of the café, standing on a small wooden stage with her eyes closed, was a woman singing. If one could call it that. It was more like high-pitched chanting. She wore a long purple skirt and her black hair was pulled into a low ponytail. A streak of white ran through the middle of her hair, like a skunk.

"I really don't think this is where I belong," Coco said solemnly.

"You don't *belong* here! You are *starting* here," Mac hissed.

"Hurray to that," Erin chimed, lifting up her coffee cup in a fake toast. In a long draw-stringed skirt with sparkly threading, Erin was the only person who actually looked like she fit in. The thought was terrifying.

"I'm not so sure," Coco whispered. She *was* sure that her life had sunk to abysmal lows. Less than a month ago, she'd auditioned for the biggest record producer in the world, and now here she was, about to perform in a coffee shop that only served earth-friendly, animal-friendly, soul-friendly coffee, according to the barista. These people were too weird for their own good.

"You have to build your fan base from the bottom up." Mac shot her an imploring look as the "singer" onstage let out a final, punctuating bleat.

Well, I've definitely found the bottom, Coco thought, as she nervously clutched her Yamaha guitar and studied her future fans. A fortyish woman with pigtails and denim overalls typed furiously on her laptop, like she was mad at the keyboard. Another woman with a long, pointy nose sat primly on the couch, knitting what appeared to be a yellow ski hat even though it was eighty degrees outside. A rail-thin man in shorts and Birkenstocks dozed in a rocking chair, rocking away.

"Do you think my mother ever played for just a few people?" Coco asked. Before Coco's mother retired, she had sold out her last three hundred stadium concerts. As a baby, Coco had traveled the world on her mother's farewell tour, hearing thousands of people screaming her mother's name.

"Of course Cardammon did!" Emily said, sipping her organic mocha from a coffee cup that said SAVE WATER, and had suspicious-looking crud on the handle. Coco wondered if "saving water" meant "not using dishwashers." Maybe dirty was the new green?

Mac, who had been e-mailing from her iPhone, snapped back into the conversation. "Babe, you gotta start *somewhere*." She looked around and waved her phone like a remote control. "And that somewhere is the Karma Café open mic night."

"I don't think these people came here to hear music." Coco noted that the only quasi-normals were two girls having coffee, chattering like they were catching up after years apart. Coco imagined how she would feel if she were at an Inner Circle reunion and suddenly interrupted by some random girl with a guitar. She *was* that random girl.

"Sometimes people don't know what they want,"

Mac said dismissively. "You're the diamond in the rough here. So go sparkle."

Coco's nerves throbbed to their own Swedish techno beat. She had to back out—how could Mac set her up like this, after all she had been through in the past month! Coco cringed thinking about her very recent Rejectapalooza:

1. After auditioning with Ruby Goldman for a record deal, the producer had decided to go with Ruby—solo. (Ow!)
2. After she'd been elected captain of the dance team, the girls had turned against her, booted her off the team, and downgraded her to water fetcher. (Double ow!)
3. At the school show, Coco had done the wrong dance in front of a sold-out crowd and gone down in school history as a total disaster. (Beyond ow!)
4. NOW THIS!

"I can't handle—" Coco began to protest.

"I'm so proud of you." Mac beamed with pride. "You have been through so much recently."

Coco's jaw dropped. Sometimes it felt like Mac could work her emotions like John Mayer playing an older woman. But then she realized—Mac was right. She *had* been through a lot, and none of the rejection had killed her. How could a potentially embarrassing gig in front of a roomful of losers hurt any more than what she had already endured?

The answer was: It couldn't.

Before Coco could utter another syllable, the barista stepped out from behind the counter and walked toward her. "Hey, I'm Finneas Grace," he said, tugging at his black vest. "But you can call me Finn." His hair was mussed up and flared around his head, making him look like a boy version of a mermaid. He looked like he had just woken up from a long sleep. Still, there was something slow and cool about him, like it took a lot to impress him.

"You ready to rock out?" Finn asked.

Coco winced, but nodded.

Finn walked up onto the stage. "Good evening, my friends." He glanced at the list on his clipboard, which was covered in PETA stickers. "Next up, please give some good karma to . . . Coco!"

Mac, Becks, Erin and Emily cheered like they were at a Justin Timberlake concert at Staples Center. The Karma regulars shot them annoyed glares.

Coco tiptoed cautiously onto the rickety platform in her two-inch heels, feeling it creak with every step. She plopped her guitar on her right leg while she adjusted the microphone so it was about three inches from her chin. Then she closed her eyes, strummed the first A-minor chord, and began to sing her "Water Boy" song. It was a silly tune she'd made up at an Inner Circle slumber party, inspired by how she'd been forced to be the water fetcher for the dance team.

I'm a sad, sad water boy
Treat me like I'm a toy
That you throw away

It was part Jonas Brothers, part Ashlee Simpson, and it was supposed to be a little bit cute and quirky (like Coco!). And she had forgotten she'd even sung it at the sleepover until days later, when Mac had convinced her to write it down.

'Cause you don't even care—

The woman with the laptop abruptly slammed it shut. She stood up and stared at Coco, shaking her head in a way that said, *You bad singer, you ruined my day.* Coco's stomach twisted into a knot, and she struggled to remember the next line. She tried to focus on her music, but all she wanted was to unhook the guitar strap and apologize to everyone for interrupting their mellow vibe with her noise.

Still, she could see the Inner Circle listening supportively. Coco owed it to them to continue. As long as there was one person in the audience, *the show must go on.* She closed her eyes and struck another A-minor chord.

Enough to say buh-bye—

And as she focused on her music, and not on the audience, something magical happened: Coco forgot about everything else. She enjoyed the feel of her fingers on her guitar, and she even *liked* singing her song. Coco sat up a little straighter and sang a tiny bit louder, and stayed in that effortless zone until the last line.

I'm just a sad, sad water boy.

When she finished, there was silence. Coco grabbed the microphone with her right hand and, in a breathy voice, said, "Thank you."

Mac, Emily, Becks, and Erin roared. But as Coco snapped back to reality, she realized that it wasn't just her BFFs: it was *everyone*. Even the crazy man in the rocking chair was smiling and giving her two thumbs up. He swayed his head, still moving to the beat that Coco had stopped singing. The two friends having the reunion had even paused to applaud. So Coco hadn't ruined everyone's day, after all.

Mac high-fived Coco as she stepped off the stage.

"Dude, that was awesome." Becks bear-hugged her.

"They *really* liked you," Emily agreed.

"You were beautiful and powerful," Erin said somberly. "It was extraordinary."

Coco grinned proudly. Her friends had seen her fail so much in the past month, and now—finally—they could see her succeed. "Yeah, and I only lost one person!" Coco joked about the computer lady.

"Aw, that's nothing!" Erin said, her green eyes twinkling. "Sometimes when I perform, half the crowd leaves."

There was an awkward pause. Mac, Emily, Becks, and Coco stared at Erin, sadly. She played the flute in a new-age music group and was devoted to changing the world through song.

Erin sighed. "Such is the life of a maverick."

Mac shook her head quickly, like she was trying to erase Erin's existence, and gripped Coco by the shoulders. "I am so proud of myself," she said, peering into Coco's almond-shaped eyes. "Because I totally called this. You are a hit!"

Coco smiled. Compliments from Mac were as rare and wonderful as secret sales at Ron Herman.

"All righty," Mac said breezily to the group. "Let's bounce. I'm allergic to being this far from the ocean." As Coco picked up her guitar, Mac swiveled on her Marc Jacobs mouse flats and headed toward the door. Emily zipped up her hoodie and followed, with Becks and Erin right behind.

Just as Coco was about to leave the coffee shop, she felt a thin hand on her shoulder. She turned. It was Finn, the cutely scrawny barista.

"Man, oh man." His eyes stared off in the distance, like he was reliving every moment of Coco's performance. "That was amazing."

Coco smiled shyly. She wasn't used to compliments from boys, let alone from boys who seemed like they were in high school, or hard to impress. In a weird way, it was even better than the compliments from her friends.

"Thanks." Coco grinned.

"You just owned it." Finn was now looking right at her. "And you're *good* on the guitar. But your voice, it's like just so unique and, like, *not* unique. Like Janis Joplin but smooth. . . ."

"Seriously, thanks," Coco purred demurely, just like she'd seen her mother do with fans. "Are you a singer too?"

"Kind of," Finn said. "I play the tambourine for Electric Hug, and I write music reviews for *L.A. Weekly*. But I'm working here after school until I graduate and can do music full-time."

Finn seemed completely unaware that Coco was trying to go. "Hey, question for you . . ."

Coco's heart began to thump. She had a feeling she was a second away from being asked out.

"You look so familiar—what's your name again?"

"I'm Coco Kingsley—"

The second the name "Kingsley" rolled off her tongue, Finn seemed to jolt awake.

"*Kingsley?*" He studied her face. Coco knew that look: It was the look that came right before someone connected her to her famous mother. And then it clicked. "Wait a hot second—your mom's *Cardammon*?"

"Yes?" Coco admitted, her heart sinking. She hated when people were only interested in her because of her mom. She'd been enjoying having accomplished something all on her own.

Finn fiddled with a button on his vest that said ANIMALS ARE FRIENDS, NOT FOOD for a really long time. Finally he shrugged. "Too bad. I thought you were more of an artist type."

"I *am* an artist type!" Coco blurted, shocked. "And so is my mom," she added, feeling defensive. *The best-selling artist of all time*, she added silently.

"Hardly." Finn just shrugged.

Coco narrowed her eyes. "So if you don't think my mother's an artist, what would you call her?" What had Cardammon ever done to him, besides nothing?

Finn ran a hand through his messy hair and pondered the question. "An entertainer?" he mused. "A celebrity?"

"Well, sure," Coco said, relieved that was her mother's only crime against humanity. "*And* she's an artist."

Finn chuckled like Coco had just insisted Santa Claus was real. "Sure, Coco. You just keep telling yourself that."

Coco's throat clamped and she tried to swallow. Okay, so maybe Cardammon's techno-Euro pop was a little manufactured—but . . . but what? Suddenly Coco felt shaken, and like she wanted to get very, very far away from Finn Grace. "I should go. . . . My friends are waiting." She turned toward the door and pushed it open. The Indian chimes overhead clanged together.

"Hey, listen." Finn tried to stop her. "I didn't mean—"

But Coco wasn't listening. She zombie-walked to the Prius and slumped into her seat.

"Sooooo . . ." Mac asked excitedly. "Does barista-boy want to book you again?"

Coco was still in shock. "Not exactly."

"Did he want a D-A-T-E?" Becks squealed. "And I don't mean for your next G-I-G!"

"I guess he wanted to tell me that my mom is lame." Coco realized that she didn't even know what his point had been. "Or that I'm not serious about music?"

"Everyone has a right to his own opinion," Erin added, saying the wrong thing as always. She started the car.

"He looks like a very troubled person," Emily offered quietly.

"Earth to Coco!" Mac commanded, cupping her hands over her mouth like a megaphone. "Emily is right. Look at him. He's just bitter that Starbucks coffee is legitimately better!"

Coco smiled, grateful for the attempts to cheer her up. But she also knew that her friends had to say those things, because that was what friends were for. Questions kept rattling around in her head as the car pulled out of the parking lot. She closed her eyes, but one question kept crashing into the back of her eyelids: Did being Coco Kingsley mean she'd never make it as an indie singer?

Her eyes snapped open. She'd always thought her mom would be embarrassed by *her*—not the other way around.

As they turned onto Sunset Boulevard, Mac turned around again to face Coco. "Besides, Cokes, Cardammon Kingsley is famous to, like, our parents. Our generation is ready for their own dose of Kingsley—*Coco* Kingsley."

Coco smiled. The night *had* gone well, minus the whole Finn thing, and sometimes critics just wanted to be critics. You could always find one person with something bad to say. She just hoped that next time the critic wouldn't be quite so cute.

cHapter FIVe

becks

◀ Saturday   September 26 ▶

6:30 AM   Jamba Juice run

7 AM   Pre-warm-up warm-up (not a typo!)

9 AM   Arrive at Manhattan Beach

10 AM   Dixie Tryouts!

Becks stood on the Manhattan Beach boardwalk and inhaled the air, which was coconut-scented and salty. The sky was clear blue, and Becks could see all the way to the Palos Verdes Peninsula. Wood-shingled beach cottages dotted the sidewalk, where rollerbladers and skateboarders breezed past. Seconds later, the tennis player Maria Sharapova jogged by in a white Nike workout dress. Becks nudged Mac to point out one of her favorite athletes, but Mac was oblivious. She hadn't looked up from her phone since they left Malibu. The girls walked down the beach in silence.

Even though Manhattan Beach was less than an hour from home, Becks had never surfed there. When you lived on a private beach in Malibu, getting in a car to go surfing was like living on a dairy farm and buying milk from the 7-Eleven. But so far the five-foot wave swells looked good—maybe too good. Suddenly Becks felt the same nervous energy as when she'd tried to surf Pipeline that summer. Mac had convinced her she was actually good enough to try to become a Dixie Gal, but now Becks wondered if she was reaching for an impossible dream.

"Becks! Mac! Over here!" Liz Dixie emerged from under a giant blue tarp that said DIXIE, wearing the same sleeveless red Patagonia from the other day. At Liz's side was Chad Hutchins, in a black Rusty tee and camouflage cargo shorts. He was devouring a stack of what appeared to be pancakes topped with bananas and whipped cream.

When they were closer to the Dixie people, Mac finally looked up from her iPhone. "It's good to see you again," she said, striking the perfect pitch of business and warmth.

"Great to see you girls," Liz chimed. Her bleached blond hair was in a ponytail and her face was shrouded by a white visor and wraparound sunglasses. "We're stoked you could make it."

"It's our pleasure." Mac grinned. "Plus we couldn't resist pancakes." Chad and Liz laughed.

"Let me tell you about how today's gonna work." Liz spoke gently. "Tryouts are really simple. Each girl surfs in the morning—"

Just then Mac's phone rang. She looked down to see who was calling, and her face scrunched in worry. "Please excuse me everyone, I have to take this." Then she turned to Becks. "Emily needs me. It's her first day of shooting—"

"Is everything okay?" Becks asked. Mac always had a lot going on, but today seemed even busier than usual.

Mac plastered on a smile. "It's all good. I just need to talk her through a few things." Without another word, she headed back to the sidewalk, phone glued to her ear.

Becks gulped watching Mac walk away, swallowing down the sour feeling. Emily needed Mac as much as she did, if not more.

Liz put an arm around Becks and walked her into the shade of the tarp. "So, as I was explaining, each girl surfs in the morning. Then there's a lunch break, and we might ask you to stick around a little longer. The real point is to just have some fun out there. Treat this like you would any other day at the beach."

Becks smiled nervously. Even though she had secretly pretended she was a Dixie Gal for years when catching waves in Malibu or San Onofre, she'd never actually expected to get a chance to try out for them. And now that she was *thisclose*—she could taste it like the salt in the Pacific—she was suddenly aware of how disappointed she'd be if she blew it. She took a deep breath and put her LeSportsac duffel down in a corner of the Dixie tent. She glanced around at the other girls trying out to be the fourth Dixie Gal. There were about ten girls, all muscular and pretty. Becks didn't recognize any of them.

But sitting in the middle of the tent, in royal blue beach chairs, were three girls whom Becks knew instantly: the Dixie Gals. Becks didn't usually spaz when Mac pointed out Hollywood celebrities, but these girls were like goddesses. In the pictures, it was hard to tell their age, but in real life they looked at least sixteen. They were sipping Charge-flavored Vitamin Waters (Dixie's sponsored drink) and holding Uno cards. They all wore royal blue polish on their toenails, Dixie's signature color. Becks smiled shyly, trying not to stare.

"Hey you!" the blondest girl called from her chair. "Are you Evangelina Becks?" She was wearing a yellow vintage *Star Wars* T-shirt, and her chin-length hair looked stylishly mussed, like she hadn't brushed it in days. Her name was Tully, and she was shockingly pretty in person: thin but muscular. Her dirty blond hair was dry like straw, and she had a ridge of freckles running across her nose.

"Yeah. Um, hey." Becks smiled, proud that Tully knew her name.

"We know all about you," said a brunette girl with a boxy body and well-defined abs. She had a gruff voice that was also a little bit masculine. Becks knew her name was Darby.

"You live in Malibu," added the third girl, Leilani, who had French braids in her black hair and the perkiness of a cheerleader. She was from Maui and had moved to the mainland two years ago to join the Dixie Gals.

Becks nodded nervously. She could feel the other ten girls watching her, probably wondering why she was being singled out.

"I'm Tallulah," the tall blond girl pointed to herself. "But don't call me that. Call me Tully." Becks nodded and pretended she didn't already know. Tully pointed to the brunette with the amazing abs. "This is Darby." Next she gestured to the girl with the French braids and insanely white teeth. "And that's Leilani. Lei loves meeting new people."

Darby smiled. "That's what—"

"—she said!" Tully finished.

All three girls laughed.

Tully smiled at Becks again. "Sometimes we—"

"—finish each other's sentences," added Lei.

"That's. . . ." Becks trailed off, wishing there was someone nearby to finish hers. She peered up at the boardwalk, hoping that Mac might be watching from one of the benches, but she couldn't see her anywhere.

"Anyway, good—" Lei started.

"—luck out there," Tully finished with a wink, before the girls went back to Uno.

Three hours later, Mac still hadn't shown and all the girls were taking an official break in the shade of the

Dixie tarp. Becks was sitting on her yoga mat, sipping a Vitamin Water. She'd given every wave her all, she thought, squeezing the last sip of her water. Now she was almost too exhausted to be nervous—her arms were aching, and her skin felt windburned—but she wanted to be a Dixie Gal more than ever.

Chad Hutchins came by to thank everyone for a great day. Becks watched as the others in her tryout group nodded and began packing their things. She held her breath, hoping that the Dixie folks weren't done with her.

Chad glanced over at her. "We want to keep you for just a little bit longer—do you mind?" Becks's heart pounded with excitement. She nodded enthusiastically. As if she needed convincing!

She reapplied some SPF 45 and reached for her board. Then she bounded into the water where the three Dixie Gals were already waiting. They'd paddled out past the breaking point and were perched like swans in the ocean, eyeing the swells. The Dixie catalog always featured glossy shots of the gals surfing in a line, so Becks knew group alignment was key. She sculled her arms underwater so she'd be ready to sprint when the moment came. Would they call out what wave they were going to take? Or would she just have to take a chance and trust her instincts?

Soon Tully's arms wound up, and even though it wasn't the wave Becks would have picked, she just *knew* it was time to make a move. *I have no idea what I'm doing and I just don't wanna be the last one to shore,* she thought as she dug into the water. There was no turning back now. She stood up and twisted her body into the wave, powering herself forward. The breeze whipped through her as she barreled to shore, and she felt light and powerful. When she stepped off her board seconds later, she saw she'd timed it perfectly with the Dixie Gals.

The girls plopped their boards in the sand, unstuck their ankle straps, and ran over to Becks. To her surprise, they *hugged* her. They were a tangle of long limbs and shiny bikinis, jumping up and down.

"We knew you could hang with us!" Tully exclaimed.

"Yay!" cheered Lei. "We totally wanted you!"

"Totes!" Darby's voice was gruff but happy.

Becks giggled. Normally she was the only one who used the word *totes.* Before Becks could say anything, Chad Hutchins sauntered over. "Good news and good news. Rock on, Becks, you're the fourth Dixie Gal." He smiled and dabbed royal blue zinc on her nose, while the other three Dixie Gals whooped. "And the second good news is that your first shoot is in a week." He held up his right hand to Becks and they high-fived.

Giddily, Becks glanced around the beach to find Mac. Good news didn't officially count until she shared it with her BFF, and she couldn't wait to hear what Mac would say about *this.* Especially since she owed everything to her. Becks scanned the beach in every direction but she couldn't spot Mac anywhere.

Becks and the Dixie Gals strolled into the tent to grab their things. "Later, skater!" Tully said. "We gotta head out, but see you next week!" Becks smiled and noticed her phone was blinking from her bag. Mac had sent her a text:

BRK A LEG BBE! HAD 2 GET 2 SET. I KNOW YOU'LL DO GR8.

Becks's shoulders fell. She couldn't believe Mac had missed it—all of it. But she was too thrilled to stay upset. *It had really happened.* Over the course of a few hours, she'd gone from everyday eighth-grader to professional surfer, calendar model, and official Dixie Gal.

She inhaled her favorite scent—the combination of surf wax and sunblock—and dove into the blue ocean water. Mac had been saying it all along, but now Becks was a believer: Nothing felt better than success.

CHAPTER SIX

mac

2:30 PM Double-check w/Chris that Emily will
have no-sugar-added caramel Iced
Blended delivered every morning
(remind him they **have** to be from
Coffee Bean—no Bucks!)

2:35 PM Call Mom to confirm protocol for agents
on set

3 PM Join Emily on set

Reminder: Check in w/Becks re: tryout
Reminder: Check in w/Coco re: next gig
Reminder: Find a nice way to ask Erin to not eat
garlic hummus in Prius?
Reminder: TAKE CHARGE!

Mac waltzed onto the *Deal With It* set, positively buzzing over how much she'd accomplished in so little time: By now, Becks was probably the fourth Dixie Gal; Coco's career was taking off; and Emily was shooting a major Hollywood movie. Mac happily recalled one of Mama Armstrong's many life rules: *Life is what you make of it.* Mac Little-Armstrong was making it a VIP party.

"Ciao bella!" she exclaimed to Emily as she barged into the trailer.

Emily was nestled in a white chair with a canvas back, surrounded by a bevy of stylists. Tina Stella (one of the best makeup artists in Hollywood) applied foundation to Emily's face with white sponges shaped like triangle blocks. A round man named Robyn (the winner of four Daytime Emmys for hairstyling) was flat-ironing Emily's wavy, cinnamon brown mane. He was about sixty, with high cheeks and pouty lips.

His blond hair was shaped like a helmet around his head.

Emily, in the middle of this circus, seemed exhausted.

Mac studied her budding star suspiciously. "Have you eaten today?"

Emily gave Mac a weak smile. "I think so. . . ."

"Don't worry!" Mac commanded, in mother-bear mode. "I know what you need." Mac knew Emily's favorite foods by now. She purposefully bounded out of the trailer and down the metal steps, where she ran . . . smack into Davey Woodward.

"Watch it, Mac Attack!" he said, rubbing a hand on his shoulder where Mac had just bumped him.

"Hi and 'bye! On a mission!" Mac smiled and started walking, barely looking at Davey. She had to be polite because Davey was her mother's biggest client, but she wasn't about to stop and chat. To her surprise, he started walking with her. "Emily's in the trailer," Mac explained, figuring he'd turn around and go back.

"I was actually on my way to see you," Davey said meaningfully. He looked like he was about to confess something serious, like he had a secret twin or horrible disease.

Mac paused, and actually looked at Davey. His skin was bronzed, making his bright blue eyes stand out even more—it was like they could see right through her. For a moment, Mac was speechless. Had he always been so cute? Why hadn't she noticed? She knew other girls went crazy for Davey—girls like Emily.

"Okay, suit yourself," she said, and kept walking. She marched past the art department offices toward the catering tent, where the food was stocked like an all-you-can-eat buffet.

Just before they reached the tent, Mac spotted Kimmie Tachman's live-blogging station. It was a pink table with a pink armchair, specially ordered by Kimmie's dad, Elliot Tachman.

"Mac!" Kimmie squealed. "Great Marc Jacobs dress! Where'd you get it?"

"Hey Kimmie," Mac said, ignoring the compliment in a bored-but-polite voice. There was nothing wrong with Kimmie; she was just a little too dorky and usually looked like she'd vomited Pepto-Bismol all over herself. Besides, she could never take sides, and sometimes batted for the Rubybots instead of for the Inner Circle. Mac hated unclear friend loyalties.

"Mac!" Kimmie fake-scolded. "You have *got* to give me an exclusive with Emily. I want to be the first reporter to get her before she becomes a megastar." Then Kimmie pointed at Davey. "And I want you, too . . . for an interview, of course."

Davey smiled, like he genuinely loved talking to the Tawker. Which was improbable, seeing as Kimmie was one of those nice-but-annoying girls who boys couldn't stand to be around because she talked way too much

57

about clothes and gossip. She was like e-mail spam: harmless, but a nuisance. "Sure thing, Kimmie," Davey said with an adorably dimpled smile.

"You know my name?" Kimmie giggled and ran her fingers through her curly hair.

"Of course! How could I not?" Davey said, oozing charisma the way most boys their age oozed BO.

"Great, when?" Kimmie asked, already flipping through her day calendar.

Mac knew this was her time to bounce. "I'll leave you two to figure out schedules," she said. "I'm on a food run."

"I'll go with you!" Davey called after Mac. "Talk to you soon, Kimmie. Let's set something up, and if I forget, be sure to remind me, okay?" And with that, he followed Mac to the food table.

Davey stood close beside Mac. She ignored her nerves and rolled up the sleeves on her Splendid cardigan. She set to work making Emily's favorite tuna sandwich: garlic mustard on onion focaccia, tuna with pickles and onions, plus a layer of potato chips in the middle. Even Mac's older brother, Jenner, who would eat anything, had been totally grossed out. He had dubbed it the Breathalyzer, but it was Emily's favorite comfort food from Iowa.

"You're quite the chef," Davey teased. He was standing so close that Mac's elbows kept brushing his tan arms. A little shiver went up her back.

Mac smiled awkwardly. "Yes, well, thanks." She clutched her sandwich and turned back to the trailer. "I should get this back to Emily."

"It's nice you support her." Davey smiled. "She's great. I'm really glad she's here—and that you are too."

"Oh," was all Mac could say. He was glad *she* was here? She gripped the paper plate tightly.

"I'm just . . ." Davey began, leaning in closer. The crocodile on his pastel pink polo shirt looked blurry. "I'm just really looking forward to spending more time with you," he whispered.

Mac jerked back in surprise. A compilation of all her D.W. interactions flashed through her mind like a movie montage. She thought of all the times he'd been over to her house to "talk about projects" with her mother, but always had a Coffee Bean Iced Blended "just in case Mac wanted one." Or the times he'd called Mac's cell phone looking for Adrienne. Or those VIP parties he'd invited Mac to attend. Did he . . . *like* her? Like *that*?

Mac felt that nervous energy again, like a tingling in her toes, and she had to admit she was . . . flattered.

But only for a millisecond.

Then the alarms blared in her head. Emily had luvved Davey since forever, and a M.L.A. + D.W. connection would be worse than L.C. and Justin betraying Audrina times a million. Mac was so shocked by this news bomb that she dropped her sandwich smack on the floor.

"Oh, shoot! I gotta make her another one!" Mac said.

She turned and practically threw the mustard onto the onion bread, ignoring Davey's speechless stare. As she speed-walked back to Emily, Mac turned over her shoulder to holler at Davey. "Let's talk later!"

It wasn't a *total* lie, but if *later* never came, that would be just fine.

CHAPTER
seven

emily

◄ Saturday September 26 ►

FIRST DAY OF SHOOT!!! I'M A REAL ACTRESS NOW!!!

RELAX POST-SHOOT (poolside at Co's, anyone?)

Emily sat in her trailer, polishing off the last bite of the Breathalyzer. She wasn't used to eating while people fussed with her hair and makeup. Ahem, correction: She wasn't used to people fussing with her hair and makeup, and had no idea if it was rude to eat while they did. But she was ravenous—she'd been so nervous about her first day of shooting that she'd forgotten to get food. She devoured the last corner of her sandwich while Tina doused her eyelashes with black mascara and Robyn tousled her bangs.

There was so much to be excited about. First of all, there was an entire crew of people waiting to film her. Plus there was a *second* crew, just to shoot behind-the-scenes footage for the DVD. And on top of all that, she was minutes away from seeing . . .

Davey.

Farris.

Woodward!

Emily studied herself in the mirror. She had an orange glow, ridiculously rosy cheeks, and poufy hair—but apparently on camera it would look just right. She hoped Davey would understand that she didn't normally wear so much makeup. She'd learned in his March interview with *Access Hollywood* that he liked the natural look.

Mac sat on the white couch behind her, reading. "I'm thinking of getting you into this." She gestured toward a dog-eared script. "You'd play Leighton Meester's little sister. *And* it's shooting in London."

Emily was about to say how amazing that sounded when the door burst open. It was Chris. He looked terrified. His face glistened with sweat and he was out of breath.

"We have—to change—the shot list—" he gasped. "Shane needs Emily on set, like, yesterday. We're starting with the last scene."

Robyn shook his blond head and waved his flat iron around. "No no no no no no!"

Tina stopped powdering Emily's face and glowered at Chris. "I can't work like this."

Robyn pointed the flatiron at Chris like a sword. "Listen—you—I forgot your name—I've spent two hours getting her ready for first scene."

"Guys!" Chris pleaded. "I'm just the messenger." He looked down at his clipboard. "Same hair and makeup as before so we're all good."

Tina and Robyn exchanged huffed glances, but they were quiet.

Chris turned to Emily. "Shane wants you to improvise, so don't worry if you don't know your lines yet."

Emily wasn't sure why it was such a disaster to everyone that they were shooting in a different order. She looked at Mac for instructions, but Mac was already packing scripts into her Balenciaga bag.

Emily turned to Chris. '"No worries, I'm ready to go!" she fibbed.

Chris looked at Emily as if she had just saved his life. "Bless you!" Then he whispered into his microphone, "Emily flying to set."

Freshly made up, Emily bounded down the trailer in white True Religion jeans and a lavender Nanette Lepore tank top, gripping Mac's arm. Tina and Robyn followed, their makeup and hair products tucked into giant black belts around their waists. They all followed Chris past the grip truck and the catering tents to a fake grassy mound that was supposed to resemble the New Hampshire countryside. Gold leaves were sprinkled everywhere. In the center was a giant white gazebo. Shane was holding a leaf to the light, as if to make sure it was the perfect hue.

"Dollface!" Shane lit up when he saw Emily.

There was insta-silence on set. Emily could feel hundreds of pairs of eyes—crew, agents, makeup artists, and extras—watching her every move. She felt like her performance had already started.

Shane turned and inspected Emily. "Love the hair! Love the makeup. Love, love, love." He clapped his hands every time he said the word *love*. "You look even better than that young lady," he added with a laugh, gesturing behind him toward the gazebo.

And there, in the gazebo, standing tall and aloof, with a half-smile on his face, was Davey Farris Woodward. Even though Davey was dressed like a girl, in a wig, white shirt, and plaid skirt, all Emily saw was tanned skin, chiseled cheekbones, and steely-eyed gorgeousness. D.F.W. was so stunning in person that it was hard to believe he was human. There was something about real-life movie stars, Emily thought. They just glowed. She wondered if someday, after the movie came out and people saw her acting opposite Davey, someone would think *she* glowed. Maybe some of his glowiness would rub off on her. Maybe when they had their kissing scene at the end of the movie. . . .

Suddenly, in a stomach flip-flopping rush, Emily remembered: *This* was the end of the movie. The scene was where Davey's character confessed he was really a guy. The scene where he took off his wig. And . . .

. . . they were supposed to *kiss* . . .

. . . and she'd just eaten . . .

. . . a tuna sandwich . . .

. . . and not just any sandwich . . . THE BREATH-ALYZER.

Emily covered her mouth like she was about to vomit. She *absolutely could not and would not* kiss Davey with fish breath!

Emily wanted to ask for gum, but she didn't want to interrupt Shane, who was rattling off directions for the next scene, *"Do what you did in the audition! Don't look right at the camera!"* Emily heard the words, but she wasn't listening. Frantically, she reached into the pockets of her jeans, checking for Orbitz that wasn't there.

"Iowa!" Shane snapped his fingers in Emily's face. "I need you to stand right in the gazebo." He pointed a finger toward Davey.

Numbly, Emily marched to position like she was walking down a gangplank. She had not even said two words to Davey since her audition, and now she was going to ruin their relationship before it began. She racked her brain for a way out of this scene. She quickly nixed fainting (too dramatic), faking a seizure (too unattractive), and feigning amnesia (too crazy).

Desperate to find Mac, Emily craned her neck to peer at the crowd of industry onlookers who had gathered to watch. She saw Giselle mumbling to herself, and Chris the PA talking into his headset. She saw the DVD crew, already filming everything. She saw the producer of *Deal With It*, Elliot Tachman, who looked like a giant teddy bear with his belly and big beard. Kimmie sat beside him, clutching her pink iBook. Seeing Kimmie, Emily gulped. Anything stupid she said or did would wind up on the Tawker's live blog. She imagined a headline about a dumb Iowa girl who knocked Davey Woodward out with her death breath. Which was all the more reason to find Mac now. But where in the Sony-world was she?

"*Quiet on set!*" Shane screamed. He walked to his director's chair, which had a canvas back with his name on it. There was a hush over the crowd and then Shane screamed "*Action!*"

Emily couldn't believe it was all happening so fast. Her heartbeat was racing. Already the cameras were filming her. Davey snapped into his character mode and faced Emily. "Look, Kelly, there's something I need to tell you—"

He began to remove the braided wig and leaned in close to kiss Emily. Even though Emily knew it was acting—make believe, pretend—her tuna breath was very, very real. Suddenly she didn't even see hotness in Davey, she just saw Code Red Terror. Between the heat, the lights, and the people staring at her, Emily felt like she was going to faint.

"Hold up!" Emily screamed. "What's my motivation?" It seemed like a clever way to show she was a serious actress, a Meryl-in-the-making, his next Oscar-winning star . . . so Emily continued. "I'd like to take this material home and work on it tonight."

Shane stared at her like she'd turned into a wildebeest. "CUT! CUT! CUT!"

She looked over at the industry crowd and saw Mac pushing her way through to the front, her blue eyes widened in horror. Mac ran over to her. "What do you think you're doing?" Everyone—even Emily—knew it was a cardinal crime to interrupt a shot. *That* was how desperate she was.

"I need breath mints," Emily whispered when Mac was close.

"I cannot believe this," Mac hissed, slipping a roll of Lifesavers into her hands.

"I'm all set!" Emily screamed big to show that she was ready to be serious. "Figured it all out." She had never felt so relieved to freshen her breath in her entire life. She turned her face away from the crowd, unrolled the entire package of mints, and shoved them all into her mouth.

"And we're going again!" Shane screamed in an exasperated voice. He took his position behind the monitor. Slowly he raised his right hand to the sky and then brought it down in one strong swoop. *"Action!"*

Davey faced Emily exactly as he'd done the first time. "Look, Kelly, there's something I need to tell you—"

Emily wanted to respond, but she'd stuffed her face with mints and now her cheeks were swollen like a chipmunk's. Davey was looking at her like she was a freak, which only made her more nervous. She tried to quickly chew her mints so she could swallow them. But the more she thought about *not* spewing mints all over Davey, the more her lips began to quiver nervously. He leaned in closer, and Emily prayed that he'd know to back off. She waved him away, but he kept coming. Then, just when he leaned in to kiss her, Emily did the only thing more heinous than unleashing her fish breath on him: She sprayed him with a mouthful of half-chewed breath mints.

"Ow," Davey said, wiping a chunk of Lifesaver off his nose.

Emily felt sick to her stomach and she ran behind a tree.

"Um, I think I need to go clean up?" Emily could hear Davey's voice calling to Shane. "Maybe Emily needs to get well?"

Shane sighed. "THAT'S A WRAP, EVERYONE," he announced.

Emily wiped her brow, and emerged from behind the fake tree. She wanted to call out, *I'm not actually sick!* But the crew began silently packing their gear, and Tina and Robyn were wiping Davey's face, talking in hushed whispers. Kimmie Tachman was looking at her sadly and the DVD crew was hoisting cameras at her. Mac was staring at her like she'd seen the apocalypse.

Emily's tongue felt like sandpaper and she stood alone in the grass. Shane flashed Emily a fake smile.

"We'll get it next time, dollface!" he yelled. But he was about as believable an actor as Paul Walker.

Emily smiled weakly. It was her first day of shooting, and so far she had disappointed Mac and—to put it mildly—made a bad impression on Davey. And then, seeing the glares on people's faces as they left the set, Emily's shoulders sank. She hadn't just made a bad impression on Davey. She'd made a bad impression on *everyone*.

The Breathalyzer had done its worst.

CHapter
EIGHT

becks

◀ Monday   September 28 ▶

12 PM Lunch with Coco

3 PM Surf Practice—work on charging those lefts

5 PM Am I the only one who can hang out these days???

"To La Table!" Becks cheered as she and Coco sidled up to their favorite table at Bel-Air Middle School. Mac had picked it out, due to its perfect balance of privacy and voyeuristic opps. Even though she and Emily were on set, Becks and Coco had to uphold tradition.

Last night, Becks had had a quickie conference iChat with Mac, Coco, and Emily, where the girls had promised to accompany her on her first international Dixie trip. Mac and Emily had had to hop off before they could say how shooting was going, but knowing those two, Emily was probably on her way to an Oscar. Then, Becks and her dad had gone to California Pizza Kitchen to celebrate, and they'd each ordered two barbecue chicken pizzas. After dinner, she'd Skyped with her friends in Hawaii. Everyone in her world who needed to know was in the loop. Well, everyone except her crush and next-door neighbor, Austin Holloway, but now that he was crushing on Ellie Parker, he was no longer in her world. Maybe on a nearby moon, but Becks was reserving her planet for the people who actually cared.

"How's your singing going?" Becks asked Coco, resisting the urge to discuss the latest Dixie Girls development uh-gain. She was still buzzing from her good news, but popped two sushi rolls in her mouth so she could actually listen to Coco's response.

Coco shrugged and took a bite of her baby zucchini and soy vegan wrap. "You should come over and tell me which new songs you like."

Becks smiled and offered an encouraging *my mouth is full but that sounds great* smile.

Before Becks could ask Coco if she was still upset about Finny, or whatever his name was, she spotted Ruby Goldman closing in on them like a hyena preparing to pounce on its prey. She wore a white tunic with sparkly embroidery over J Brand jeans with Mystique sandals, and was flanked by two other girls wearing the exact same outfit: Ellie Parker and Haylie Fowler. Ruby and Ellie were bouncy blondes, while Haylie Fowler was a bigger brunette, the token B-level cute girl. In any other city, she might have been A-level cute, but in L.A. the bar was just too high. Becks had dubbed them the Rubybots because they talked, thought, and dressed the same.

"Here's a flyer for you, Becksie," Ruby said, dropping a hot pink paper on Becks's tray like she was sprinkling pixie dust.

"Cool," Becks said, as neutrally as possible. It would be friend-cheating to be too nice to Ruby.

"And don't think I forgot you, Coco." Ruby placed another flyer on Coco's tray with the same annoying flourish. "I'm hosting a dance next week at the Bel-Air Bay Club for my first event as social chair."

"Cool," Coco said, showing exactly no emotion. She pulled her dark brown hair into a ponytail.

"The Decemberists are going to perform." The Ruby-bots smiled proudly.

"Sorry," Coco sighed. "We have plans."

"Cancel them," Ruby said, as though she had veto power.

"Sure thing, let me get my phone," Coco said sarcastically. She shot Becks a *help me out here* look.

"Umm . . ." Becks stammered. "Coco's right. We have a lot going on." Becks wished she could start over again before she'd even finished. She didn't sound busy, she just sounded nervous. Which, of course, she was.

"Really? *You* have a lot going on?" Ruby placed her hands on her hips while she waited for more information. As everyone in Hollywood knew, information was power.

Coco and Becks exchanged a conspiratorial look. It was Mac's job to run PR, and without her, neither girl was sure how much they should (or should not) leak about their news.

"I don't want to talk about it," Coco said. She

took a sip of her kombucha and smiled mysteriously. "Besides," she added proudly, "it's got nothing to do with BAMS."

"Fiiiine, I'll find out eventually," Ruby said fake-sweetly. "And by then I won't care. Oh, wait, I already don't."

"Super," Coco said, although she didn't sound as confident as Becks would have hoped. Mac was the one who usually stood up to Ruby, battling her back with clever comebacks and sassy one-liners. Not things like *super*. Her Dixie Gals high was slowly deflating.

"B-T-dubs, I hear your little friend Emily had a great first scene on set today," Ruby added. "And by *great* I mean *she vomited all over Davey Woodward*."

Becks shot Coco a nervous glance, but Coco just arched a perfectly plucked eyebrow and stared at Ruby suspiciously. Coco could say more with her eyebrows than most people could say with words. Becks checked her phone for an update, but all was quiet on the text front.

"Guess some people don't read the live blog." Ruby smirked.

"Sorry, we'd rather get our intel from the star herself," Coco snapped. "Not some second-rate gossip blog."

Suddenly Ruby turned to face Becks. "Hey, how's Austin?" she fake-smiled, her eyes slanted like a snake's.

Becks pursed her lips in frustration. Couldn't they at least be frenemies? Like Blair and Serena? Or Lauren and Audrina? Anything was better than this attack. "I don't know how Austin is," Becks said flatly. "I don't see him too much these days."

"Oh, I forgot!" Ruby pretended to be surprised. "'Cause he's seeing Ellie."

"Ruby!" Ellie giggled, and swatted her friend.

Becks stared down at her bento box. The excitement bubble over the Dixie Gals popped and was gone.

"Later, haters." Ruby turned sharply on her sandal, taking the Rubybots with her.

When they were finally out of sight, Becks held her hand up to her burning cheeks. After feeling like everything was going right, seeing Ruby and Ellie was like surfing in NorCal with no wet suit—a total shock to her system. A reminder of how screwed up her life actually was: Austin didn't want to see her. The Inner Circle was separated. And all her other BFFs lived in Hawaii. Becks's mental list-making ended abruptly as the lunch bell rang.

"See ya, sweets." Coco air-kissed in Becks's direction, grabbing her camel leather luggage bag as she tugged her navy RL mini skirt. Then she dashed off to class.

Becks watched as Coco disappeared among the throngs of BAMS students, some familiar-looking, others not. She had never realized how much she depended upon Mac for her social life. Why hadn't she made more of an effort with her other classmates all these years?

Standing alone at La Table, Becks scrolled through the contacts in her phone, wondering who she could possibly call. Her finger landed on a picture of the Inner Circle, and she pressed the little text button to type: WHAT R U GUYS DOING AFTER SCHOOL? PINKBERRY?

She pressed send, and three replies came almost instantly:

COCO: SORRY BÉBÉ, GOING TO PROVE FINN WRONG. XO!

EMILY: RECOVERING FROM DISASTER YESTERDAY. WILL TELL U LATER. SIGH . . .

MAC: PINKBERRY IS BANNED. LET'S ALL PRETEND DAIRY DOES NOT EXIST.

What was left of Becks's good mood was quickly evaporating like fog on a Malibu morning. She typed back to Mac, RIGHT! HOW ABOUT SOMETHING ELSE? and silently wished for Mac to write back, COME TO MY HOUSE AFTER SCHOOL! Or even, MEET ME AT THE GROVE. *That's* how desperate she was feeling: She was willing to shop. Her iPhone vibrated in her hand.

MAC: IS EVERYTHING OKAY WITH DIXIE!?!?

Becks' shoulders slumped and her heart felt heavy in her chest. It definitely wasn't the response she was hoping for. But then, that gave her an idea. She pressed reply and quickly tapped the screen of her phone: ALL GOOD. DON'T WORRY ABOUT ME. L8R.

chapter
nine

mac

◀ Monday   September 28 ▶

4 PM On-set math class

5 PM Fix you-know-what with you-know-who.
(Easier said than done. 'Nuff said.)

Reminder: TAKE CHARGE!

Mac sat in an oak-paneled classroom, half reading *Variety* and half listening to the tutor. The set was a New England boarding school classroom, with eighteenth-century reproduction paintings of colonial heroes on the walls and hollow leatherbound books lining the shelves. Davey sat on Mac's right side and Emily sat on her left, which meant that Mac was literally stuck in the middle. The rest of the class was an odd mix: There was Emily's stand-in, Sidnie, whose only job was to stand under lights while the crew adjusted them until Emily came in to film her take; and there was Kimmie Tachman, who had her pink iBook open, probably live-blogging this thrilling scene. Even the teacher was odd: Her name was Christine Calmet (pronounced "Call-*may*"). She was a large woman who wore khaki-colored shorts, a sleeveless sweat-dotted silk blouse with a big bow around the neck, and a visor, even though they were indoors.

"Who can tell me what's *interesting* about the Pythagorean theorem?" Ms. Calmet looked eagerly around the room, as if prepared to fend off answers. She anxiously tapped her fingers on the heavy oak desk. Her bare shoulders slumped forward. "Please, someone answer me?"

Davey wrote a note on a piece of paper and slid it over for Mac to see. *Um, nothing?*

Mac giggled and caught Davey's eye. Something fluttered in the pit of her stomach, and she quickly looked away, reaching for the pencil in the ridge of her oak desk. She pulled at it, but it was glued down—right, it was a prop. Davey seriously needed to stop being so flirty, and she seriously needed to stop, well, liking it.

Ever since Davey's confession, she'd been living in fear. After all, if he was forward enough to just come out and basically say that he liked Mac (who does that?!), what was to stop him from saying something around Emily?

"What are you laughing about?" Emily whispered. She looked over Mac's shoulder at Davey, trying to make eye contact.

"Nada." Mac gently shushed Emily. Emily looked annoyed but sat back in her chair.

Ms. Calmet sighed, pulling a crumpled tissue from her navy blue pleather purse. Mac wondered if she was going to cry, but then she stuck it down her shirt, mopping the sweat off her chest. "Does anyone even *know* the Pythagorean theorem?"

Mac felt bad for the tutor. She'd already once tried to write on the board, only to discover the chalk was a prop, too. "A squared plus B squared equals C squared," Mac answered obediently. "I guess it's interesting because it means you can solve triangles."

"Great, thank you Mackenzie," Ms. Calmet said enthusiastically. She was smiling hugely, like she was thirteen instead of thirty. She reached into her desk and pulled out a sheet of gold stars. She unpeeled one and ran over to stick it on Mac's new Anthropologie halter dress. Ms. Calmet was nutty, but at least she was nicer than the BAMS algebra teacher, Mrs. Earley, who gave pop quizzes that made up 25 percent of your grade.

"A star for the star behind the star!" Davey sing-songed, leaning toward Mac. He actually had a nice voice.

"Don't be rude," Mac scolded him. Ms. Calmet was a freak, but even freaks deserved to be treated like people.

"Anything for the lady," Davey said gallantly, and at that he sat up straighter and was quiet.

Emily tapped Mac on the shoulder. "What are you guys talking about?"

"Nothing," Mac mouthed to Emily and glanced down at her paper. It was covered in doodles of flowers and hearts and Davey's name. Emily's pen glided around the page, drawing a big pink heart around the words "Davey + Emily." Mac rolled her eyes. While there hadn't been any drama since Tuna-Day (aka the Breathalyzer Bomb) Emily's Daveymania compounded with Davey's Attackamac was making her feel like a shaken Diet Coke.

"Would you mind signing my Hollywood scrapbook?" Ms. Calmet interrupted Mac's mental image of an exploding soda can. "I like to take pictures of all my students." She reached into her desk and pulled out a disposable camera and a red notebook.

"No problem." Davey smiled sweetly at Ms. Calmet, turning his paper toward Mac so she could see his latest note. *Does she work for TMZ?*

Mac smiled, but this time she didn't laugh aloud. She would not encourage Davey. Just then, a text arrived from Emily.

WHAT R U GUYS TALKING ABOUT?

Mac bit her Benetinted lip. What could she say? Explaining the non-joke would just be silly. But saying "nothing" would seem suspicious, and the last thing Mac needed was Emily knowing that Davey liked her—not her best friend. Not to mention her biggest client.

There was text silence for several seconds, so Mac assumed that they had moved on, until her phone buzzed again.

R U IGNORING ME?

Mac rolled her eyes. It was hard enough to manage

Davey; she needed Emily to trust that she was on Team Ems. And if she was going to text, it might as well be for something *fun*, not a borderline-psychotic crush.

NOTHING!!! Mac shot back.

THEN WHY DIDN'T U SAY SO?

That was the final straw. Emily's crush was officially making her a nutcase. It was time to run Emterference, Mac decided. Her budding star needed a mental make-over, stat. And as her agent, not to mention her two-months-older and therefore wiser friend, it was her job to take charge of this situation. "Excuse me, may I go to the bathroom?" Mac asked.

Ms. Calmet nodded, and returned to writing on the blackboard, this time with a working piece of chalk. Mac reached over and grabbed Emily's elbow, dragging her through double doors that deposited them in the sound-stage for *Alien World Wars*, starring Andy Samberg and Sean William Scott. Mac and Emily stood on a moon set, in front of a giant green screen. Aliens milled around, and Andy Samberg, dressed as an astronaut, waved at the girls.

Mac moved over to the corner and held up her iPhone to Emily like a stop sign. "You have *got to cool it, amigo!*" she commanded. "I'm putting the kibosh on Daveytalk right now."

Emily shook her head in confusion. "Why?"

"Earth to Emily!" Mac hollered. "Time to focus on your work!"

"I'm getting good grades!" Emily stammered. The green screen gave her skin a Shrek-y glow, like she was going to be sick.

"I'm not talking about *class*," Mac sighed, realizing Emily was still thinking like a civilian instead of a star. Mac pushed her blond hair behind her ears and thought for a second. She knew that Davey liked *her*, which really wasn't surprising if you thought about it, but still—she didn't want Emily to get hurt. Even more than that, she wanted Emily to live up to her Anne Hathaway potential. She lowered her voice. "Listen, you're acting like a starstruck fan instead of a star. You need to snap out of it!"

Emily's deep brown eyes widened, and Mac knew she was somewhere between *making a point* and *being mean*. But she took it up another notch, because she needed this to stop. "You cannot act like a crazy fan from Kansas around Davey. Yes, I get you didn't want to kiss him with bad breath, but this is getting to be too much. . . ." She and Emily had already discussed what happened that first day of shooting, but Mac was beginning to suspect something similar might happen again. "I don't want to have to babysit you."

Emily stopped fiddling with her zipper. "What do you mean *babysit*?"

"Let me be frank," Mac said, as if she'd been tiptoeing up till now. "I signed up to work with Emily Skylar. You've got to leave Emily Mungler behind." She spoke like she was doing Emily a favor, which she was: She was protecting Emily from herself.

Finally, Emily sighed, like she was giving in. "You're right," she said sadly. "I can't think straight when I'm around Davey. And my career is bigger than my crush." Emily pulled her right hand out of the pocket of her Forever 21 hoodie and held it up like she was taking an oath. "I promise not to go Davey-crazy. And from now on you won't have to remind me that I'm Emily *Skylar*," she finished. There was a flash of determination in her brown eyes, and she seemed to be pep-talking herself into it.

Mac sighed in relief. She wanted to hug Emily, but also wanted to stay profesh. Sometimes being a bestie would have to come second to being an agent. This was just one of those times. "Thanks, babe," she said simply. "I knew I could count on you."

"No, thank *you*," Emily said genuinely, her sweet brown eyes looking positively doe-like. "For watching out for me."

Mac just nodded and ushered Emily back to class. But Emily's earnest thank-you made Mac feel weirdly unsettled, like she'd had Pinkberry after her weeks-long ban. It was true: Mac *was* watching out for Emily. She was helping her career, and she was saving her from possible, even probable, rejection. But a niggling voice at the back of Mac's head kept telling her there might be other reasons she wanted Emily to stay away from Davey. . . .

As they exited the moon setting and stepped back inside the boarding school, Davey glanced up from his desk. His hair fell over one blue eye and he offered Mac a subtle, barely there wink. If she didn't know better, she would have thought he was just blinking. Or just being friendly.

But as the butterflies once again took flight in her belly, she realized something with a jolt.

She liked Davey too.

And there was no theorem that solved love triangles.

CHAPTER
Ten

COCO

◀ Monday   September 28 ▶

3:30 PM   Prep for Café Pick Me Up

4 PM   Erin picks me up ☺

6:30 PM   Performance No. 2

C oco stood in her white marble bathroom at the King Bel-Air Hotel, a five-star hacienda off Stone Canyon Road. Her father was the hotel mogul Charles Kingsley, who owned five-star properties around the world and kept residences in all of them. The top floor of the Bel-Air outpost had been her home for as long as Coco could remember.

In her white marble bathroom, Coco put the final swooshes of blue mascara on her eyelashes. To rid herself of the Rubybot energy after today's lunchtime encounter, she had changed into a Kate Moss for Topshop minidress, black beret, and silver ankle-boots—all bought during a weekend jaunt to her father's London hotel. As she appraised herself in the mirror, she randomly wondered if Finn Grace would think it was too brand name–y or not artsy enough. But then she was annoyed at herself for even thinking of him.

Tonight was her debut at a new coffee shop (at least,

it was new to Coco), called Café Pick Me Up—which, Erin assured her, always got a huge crowd of people who understood music. Unlike Finn. So what if he thought her mother ruined music? First of all, Cardammon's songs were legendary, and okay, maybe they were a tad over-the-top, but what did that have to do with Coco anyway? She was indie. She was artsy. She was her own woman, hear her roar.

Her phone buzzed with a text from Erin:

IM DOWNSTAIRS, BEHIND SWAN POND.

Coco spritzed herself with one final dash of Agent Provocateur and took dainty steps on the green carpet leading to her front door. But on her way out, she saw the door to her private dance studio was mysteriously open. Her mother's voice floated down the hallway, along with laughter from strangers. What was going on? Cardammon only used the room for her yogalates classes in the mornings, and it was four o'clock in the afternoon.

Curious, Coco peered inside the studio. There, in a floor-length purple sequin gown, was Cardammon, nibbling at a biscotti while two young stylists pinned her dress. It was strapless and tightightight to the knees, where it fanned out in a dramatic flourish. Her mother looked like a cross between Disco Barbie and Barney. A man who Coco recognized as her mom's old choreographer was holding up a small DVD player with a screen for Cardammon to watch.

Coco's French bulldog, Madonna, was nuzzled against Cardammon's foot in a matching purple dog dress. Seeing Coco, Madonna yapped loudly.

"And there's my beautiful daughter!" Cardammon pointed her half-eaten biscotti at Coco like a wand. Her face was coated in makeup so thick that Coco imagined writing her initials in the foundation. Suddenly, five pairs of eyes were staring at her. The choreographer looked Coco up and down, as if evaluating her potential.

"Baby Cardammon!" cooed one of the stylists, a twentysomething blonde with hair down to her butt.

"No, luv, that's *Coco*," Cardammon corrected. She waved away the stylists working on her train, and turned to her daughter. "Darling, I have a little surprise for you," she said, stepping down from the platform. Behind her, her minions stood at attention. "Now, I know I said I was retired for good, but they've worn me down. I'm making a comeback!"

Coco turned her head to the side, as though that might help her make sense of what she'd just heard. Her mother . . . was planning . . . a *comeback*? Her eyes darted around the room. There were freestanding clothing racks scattered all over the dance studio, overflowing with outfit choices: silver and gold armor, leather pants with glittering laces down the legs, a tail of peacock feathers, a yellow feather boa, a gown that seemed to be made of lightbulbs. . . .

"I'm back, darling!"

Coco gulped. Cardammon was back all right. And tackier than ever.

At Cardammon's announcement, the stylists began applauding. One of them pushed a button on the remote and "Forever Blue," her mom's hit single from the '90s, began playing over the studio's sound system. "I was never convinced the timing was right," Cardammon continued, waving her fingernails, which were also painted an iridescent purple. "But you know what they say: Forty is the new twenty. . . ."

Coco glanced at the small screen her mom's choreographer was holding up, and realized in horror that it was a mock-up of the choreography for the show. She glimpsed shirtless male dancers, a human pyramid, and some Pussycat Dolls–like shimmying before she finally turned away. *This* was exactly what she was trying to get away from.

Her mother kept talking. "I know I said I was glad you'd given up on pop stardom," Cardammon said, a hopeful glint in her eyes, "but I've been thinking about it, and I'd love for you to do the finale in my reunion tour." She held up a purple sequined gown in Coco's size—it was an exact replica of the monstrosity she was now wearing. The gown hung there limply, like a bedazzled purple puddle. "What do you say, luvvy?"

Coco pictured herself wearing the dress in front

of thousands and thousands of her mom's fans. Was Cardammon's idea of mother-daughter bonding international humiliation? She took a deep breath, readying herself to say she was actually thinking of taking her sound in a different direction, when suddenly the choreographer pumped up the volume on the "Forever Blue" remix and a techno beat filled her eardrums. The base rattled the floor and her mom's electronic whine screamed through the speakers.

"This is your part, luv!" her mom yelled. "We're going to update the sound for the new era. It's white hot! Can you feel it?"

Coco could feel it, all right. She could feel Finn's words washing over her like a wave, and for the first time the feeling nagging at her took hold and expanded in her mind like one of those magic capsules that grows in water.

Cardammon began moving her arms in weird circles, gyrating her hips in her purple sequined dress. In the '90s, one of her videos had started a dance craze called the Flame, but now it just looked pathetic and dated. *Like my mom*, Coco thought sadly. Even if she was the biggest star in the world a lifetime ago—Coco's lifetime to be exact.

"Thanks, Mom, but. . . ."

Cardammon reached for the remote and turned the music off abruptly.

"But what?" she asked, a look of shock taking over her face. "I thought you wanted to be a musician?"

Coco gulped. She did. Just not with her mom. But how could she say that? There was only one answer: She couldn't. "You know, the whole performing thing just isn't for me. . . . Listen, I have to go, but congrats, really."

Cardammon's pointed shoulders fell dejectedly. "Where are you off to?"

"I'm just checking out a coffee shop," Coco answered. "It's called Pick Me—" Coco stopped herself, realizing that she'd just told her mother that she was done performing. She reached for another lie.

"I promised Mac I'd work with her. We, um, have a project for school."

Madonna growled disapprovingly and Coco made a mental note to Google "dog instincts."

Cardammon swooped down to pick up Madonna and placed a fat kiss on Madonna's adorably smushed face, leaving lipstick marks. "Well, give that girl some sugar from me."

"Mwah, love you." Coco waved to her mother and flitted out the door, surprised at how easy it was to lie to someone who trusted you.

Coco stood at the side of the stage at Café Pick Me Up in Echo Park, sizing up the crowd. Everyone seemed to have that Finn Grace look—kind of scraggly, semi-tight jeans, and androgynous haircuts. They looked like they needed a grooming intervention, Coco thought. Then she stopped herself. These were *her* people now. She hoped she could learn to love the look.

Coco was about to sing her first song, "Water Boy," and she was already out of breath. Her body had raced with nervous energy ever since leaving Bel-Air. She felt guilty about lying to her mother, and she was jittery about performing. She couldn't even eat a Larabar. No wonder rock stars were so skinny.

When her name was called, Coco nervously gripped her guitar and walked slowly onto the red Persian carpet that was, apparently, the stage. The crowd gave her a few weak claps. No one seemed to notice, or care, that she was up there hoping to get their attention.

"Hello. I'm Coco," she began timidly, looking into the crowd. A few tables in, a young woman pointed to the magazine she was reading and whispered something to her friend. From there it looked like a game of telephone, as she whispered something to the man behind her, who whispered something to someone else.

Coco strummed the opening chord of her song, when finally someone said, "Coco *Kingsley*!?"

"Sing 'On Fire for You'!" someone else yelled from the darkness.

"'Forever Blue'!" another voice called out. It felt like a small hipster army was making fun of her.

Coco looked down at her silver boots, wishing she could click them together and vanish. She wanted to cry out, *But I'm not Cardammon and you never gave me a chance!* But what was the point? These people—*her* people—thought she was a joke.

To: Emily Mungler
From: Davey Farris Woodward Fan Club
Subject: Your membership

We are sorry to hear that you would like to cancel
your subscription to the Davey Club. After five years
as an active member, we'd appreciate your filling
out the following survey question:

So we can do a better job for Davey fans, would
you please let us know why you are canceling?
(Please check all that apply)

☐   New star crush
☐   Didn't hear back from Davey
☐   Didn't ♥ Davey's last movie
■   Other (please explain): <u>Ruining my career.</u> ☹

chapter
eleven

◀ Monday September 28 ▶

7 PM Sloopy's with the girls (the new girls)

Becks and the Dixie Gals were sitting in a shady garden at Sloopy's in Manhattan Beach. After getting Mac's text at lunch, Becks had called Tully, who'd invited her to hang out without a moment's hesitation. She'd insisted they go to Sloopy's because they had the best burgers in SoCal. Even better than In-N-Out, apparently.

So far, each girl had already gone through a cheeseburger, a basket of fries, and a milk shake, and there was an extra milk shake in the middle of their table. They had already covered the great long vs. short surfboards debate (short!), listed reasons why Huntington Beach was actually a better place to surf than Oahu (closer, fewer tourists, no coral), and why yoga was so important to their training (best way to stay limber on a board). Becks had never had these kinds of conversations with girlfriends before—the closest she got to talking about waves with the Inner Circle was whether wavy really was the new straight or if that was just what curly-haired magazine editors wanted you to think.

"Hey Becks, we need you to settle a little argument for us." Tully tucked her starchy dry hair behind her ears. Becks could almost hear Mac's voice, urging Tully to deep-condition.

"Oooh, I know what you're going to ask her!" Lei took a sip of the chocolate milk shake in the middle of the table.

Darby burped, and Becks smiled in surprise. Usually she was the one who burped in public. "Okay," Tully said invitingly. "Our question is . . ."

Becks tried to gulp down her nervousness with some of the communal milk shake. What if they were going to talk about kissing? Becks had never kissed a boy, and she wasn't ready to divulge that tidbit. Or maybe they were going to ask her whether she preferred shopping on Robertson or Montana? Her Westside friends thought those streets were a true test of character.

"Where would you rather surf?" Tully asked seriously. "Puerto Escondido or San Onofre?"

The answer was so obvious that Becks actually forgot to think before she replied. "Escondido, duh," Becks answered. That beach had the best surfing in North America.

"I tolja I liked her!" Darby screamed. She hit Lei on the shoulder. Darby was so muscular, it probably hurt, but Lei just giggled.

"You said San Onofre, wench!" Tully cried. She reached over to Lei's plate and took the last burnt french fry.

"I like Escondido." Lei smiled at Becks encouragingly.

"We *all* like Escondido," Tully said, settling the argument once and for all.

Becks let out a deep sigh of relief. Apparently she'd passed her first test. Then she took a final bite of burger and smiled. She couldn't believe that she had friends who even *knew* about the Mexican surf spot.

"I like her so much better than Tiana!" Tully sighed.

"No joke!" Lei nodded, adoringly.

"Who's Tiana?" Becks asked with a half-full mouth, pretty sure that had been the name of the fourth Dixie Gal before her.

"Hmmm . . . Tiana. . . ." Tully mused. "How do we explain Tiana?"

"Rhymes with *witch*?" Lei offered.

"Just like . . . totally high maintenance," Darby commented as she reached for the communal shake. "More drama than *The Hills*. That's why she couldn't hang with us."

Tully gave Becks a sneaky smile as if to confirm that she was off to a better start. "But we've decided you're going to be our lil' sis."

The girls smiled at each other, as though they'd been debating when to tell Becks.

Becks smiled shyly. She didn't want to ruin the moment, so she didn't say anything.

"So, are you psyched for the shoot next week?" Darby asked, stealing the last fry from Lei's plate.

"About that . . ." Becks bit her bottom lip. "What are we supposed to wear? Chad said to just show up and 'be authentic.'"

"That's what she said!" Lei joked, ignoring Becks's question.

"You're not even saying it right!" Darby swatted her friend's shoulder again. She turned back to Becks. "It's cute how you're all worried. You're like . . . shy."

"Oh, shoot," Tully said, looking at her watch. "The movie starts in, like, ten minutes. Ready, chicas?"

"Wait up! I need to do my makeup!" Lei squealed. Becks relaxed into her seat, expecting this to take a while. Okay, so she still didn't know what to wear to the shoot, but if all she had to do was be herself, she'd be fine, right? A breeze sailed past and she closed her eyes and inhaled the ocean air. When she opened her eyes, Lei was putting the cap on a tube of Burt's Bees lip balm. "Okay. Let's go."

Becks chuckled quietly to herself as she stood up. No one was talking about dominating Hollywood or shopping. In fact, Becks was pretty sure that they'd chatted about surfing for an hour straight. She thought back to lunch at BAMS, about how even though she and Coco had been friends forever, they hadn't really . . . *talked*. It was different when Mac was there, but maybe that was just because Mac could carry on a conversation with herself for hours.

"Come on, little sis!" Tully called.

Becks watched as her new friends hopped on a board lying in the sand, pretending to surf. They looked silly and funny, like the big sisters Becks had never had. Mac used to say she was like a big sister to her and Coco, on account of being generally more mature and naturally more adult (her words, of course), but watching the Dixie Gals high-five and then hug, Becks wondered if maybe it wasn't time for a new family. . . .

chapter
TWELVE

emily

3:30 PM   Private training session with Valerie Waters

4:30 PM   Private acting class with Larry Moss

5 PM   Review lines!

6 PM   Hair & makeup

7 PM   Shoot rugby scene

New mantra: ACTRESS FIRST

E mily tried to sit still in the hair and makeup trailer while Robyn straight-ironed her cinnamon-colored hair and Tina dabbed concealer under her eyes. Nervously, Emily chewed on her tenth Altoid of the day. Ever since The Breathalyzer Incident, her mouth was perma-minty. Mac sat on the couch, reading scripts that had been sent to Initiative Agency for Emily's consideration. It was hard to believe that people were already thinking about her next film—all she wanted was to get through this one.

But, Emily pep-talked herself, she *would* get through. All she had to do was focus. *Focus, focus, focus.* It was tough, fighting with your feelings all the time, but after Mac's lecture, Emily had come up with a list of ways to get over Davey:

Cancel her D.F.W. fan club membership. (Totally heartbreaking, but she'd done it!)

Refuse to look at him when they walked past each

other on set. (Well, she hadn't seen him yet, but she was totally *planning* on looking away.)

Stop writing Emily Woodward on her notebook. (Done! Made easier by Mac reminding her there was no point in a name change. "Everyone thinks of Courteney Cox, not Courteney Cox-*Arquette*," she said with a shudder.)

Emily flipped through the pages of the script they were shooting that day. It was the first real scene that Shane had decided to attempt since the Breathalyzer incident, and she wanted to prove she wasn't a lovestruck girl—or someone with a spitting problem.

She took a deep breath and murmured her lines to herself. The next scene was her character's big "aha!" moment. It was supposed to occur when she collided with Davey on the rugby field with a mouthful of mud, and wondered why his body felt so ... solid ... so ... like a guy's. It was actually very tricky to shoot because it involved falls and collisions on the rugby field. Emily had spent a whole day practicing with stunt people. She'd been instructed how to tilt her head so that the other actors could leap over her without killing her.

"Shane is a madman," Tina announced as she dabbed highlighter on Emily's cheekbones.

"I had a friend who did costumes when Shane directed that TV show *MagicKids*," Robyn said, waving the hair spray can. "She ended up having a total nervous breakdown and left the business," he stage-whispered. "She moved to Berkeley to be a paralegal."

Emily took a deep breath. If she didn't break her Davey addiction, *she* could wind up as one more Hollywood casualty. But before Emily could hyper-dwell on that thought, there was a knock at the door.

Chris appeared, and led Emily to the giant rugby field. On one side were white-painted bleachers filled with extras dressed as boarding school students on a cool fall day. At the end of the field was a giant score-board. It was still hard to believe this entire *world* had been built just for this scene.

By now Emily was used to seeing hundreds of crew waiting for her, but she still wasn't used to see-ing D.F.W. in the flesh. He wore a girl's yellow rugby outfit and was practicing throwing underhanded. He giggled and covered his mouth demurely every time he tossed the ball. Sigh. Even as a cross-dresser, he was adorable.

Mac tapped her on the shoulder. "Have fun out there," she said, with one eyebrow cocked. Emily knew that was Macspeak for *Don't screw up again.*

Emily plastered a confident smile on her face and marched over to the center of the field, where Davey and Shane were waiting.

"Okay, Buttercup," Shane began. He pointed at Davey. "This is where you find out there's something *off* with your BFF. So give us mystery, intrigue, plus suspense in those gorgeous eyes. Got that, Sweet Pea?"

"Yep," Emily said very seriously, trying her hardest to not look at Davey. She shook her shoulders, which she always did to tap into her acting zone. Then she closed her eyes, took three deep breaths, and stared at the dewy grass. She imagined a cool fall breeze, even though it was eighty-five degrees. And then, just as she'd hoped, she forgot about Davey and the cameras and the lighting crew, and in an instant—poof! Suddenly, she wasn't in Los Angeles anymore; she was a girl at a New Hampshire boarding school who wanted to play rugby with her new best friend.

Emily grabbed the ball and ran toward the crowd, just as they'd rehearsed.

"Wait!" Davey cried, running after her.

Emily darted between two players, perfectly on cue, and then—as she dove to the ground like she'd practiced—she felt two big arms encircle her. In one fell swoop, Davey grabbed her waist and they both tumbled to the ground. They wound up in the field with their heads perfectly aligned for their close-up.

"You got me!" Emily-as-Kelly laughed. Davey was pressed against her so close she could hear him breathe. It felt wonderful, but she forced herself to just focus on the scene.

She leaned in closer, watching the sapphire flecks in Davey's eyes twinkle. For a millisecond, the real

Emily wanted to giggle excitedly, but she pushed those thoughts out of her head and looked at him suspiciously, staying in character.

"Got you!" Davey squealed in the fake falsetto he was using for his role as Tiffany.

Still acting, Emily crinkled her brow. There was something . . . curious . . . something distinctly masculine about her friend Tiffany. She studied him, intrigued.

But as Kelly looked into Tiffany's eyes, searching for answers, something snapped in Emily. Just like that, she wasn't in character anymore. She was Emily, looking into Davey's eyes, feeling a connection so real there was no way they were acting. What she felt was love. And you couldn't fight love.

"*Cut!*" Shane barked. He danced a jig in the mud. "*We got it!*" And then he looked at the crew, smiling broadly. "*That's a wrap!*"

The crew and the extras began clapping. Davey stood up and helped Emily to her feet, offering her a shy smile.

"I think they liked us." He leaned over, whispering so close to her cheek that she could feel his warm breath.

That was when she realized the crew and the extras were clapping for *her*. Well, for *them*. Because she and Davey had nailed the scene—together. Because they were a team. Like GyllenSpoon, or VanEfron. She imagined what *Us Weekly* would call her and Davey: *Sky-Ward?*

"Brilliant, Dollface, just brilliant!" Shane beamed at her. "I love it when things go great!"

And I love it when they go great in front of Davey, Emily thought. Davey took off his wig and shook out his messy dark hair. He took off his girl's shirt to reveal a soft, faded gray tee. In a second, Davey went from hot to mega-hot, and Emily's nerves sizzled.

Davey held up his right palm. "High fives," he cheered.

Emily pressed her palm against his and tried hard not to hold it there forever.

"Hey, you doin' anything tomorrow night?" Davey asked when she slid her hand away. "I wanted to talk to you about something. . . ."

Emily doubled-blinked and hoped she was still a good enough actress to hide her inner freak-out. *Had Davey just asked her out on a date?* "I don't think so. . . ." she said, as casually as she could. Like she would ever not be free for D.F.W. She sneaked a covert glance at Mac, who was talking to Elliot Tachman. Emily breathed a sigh of relief.

"Great." Davey nodded. "I was thinking we could swing by Disneyland."

"Disneyland?" Emily asked. In her world, that wasn't a place you "just swung by." That was a place you maybe went once in your lifetime after months of begging, pleading, and planning. Her heart was fluttering at hummingbird speed.

"I go there sometimes to blow off steam," Davey shrugged. He looked sheepish, like he was actually worried she might laugh at him. "So what do you say?"

Emily's eyes darted to Mac once again, but now she was behind a screen watching a playback of the take. She looked pleased—and more importantly, distracted.

"Sounds cool," Emily said casually, delivering her second-best performance of the day. "I can't wait."

CHapTer
THirTeen

COCO

◀ Tuesday   September 29 ▶

6 PM   Chocolate pedicures at Bliss

7 PM   (Soy) milk and cookies at Didi Reese

M ac and Coco sat in the plush white chairs of Bliss spa in Westwood on Tuesday night. It was down the road from Bel-Air, near the UCLA campus. After Coco's Café Pick Me Up disaster, Mac had insisted a double chocolate pedicure and mud mask were in order, not to mention a major agent/friend check-in.

"They hated me the second I got onstage!" Coco wailed. She took a bite of a chocolate-dipped strawberry while a woman in a baby blue T-shirt painted her toenails bubble-gum pink. Coco had been too distraught to sleep the night before. She'd stayed up until 4 a.m., writing songs about being misunderstood. All she could think was that her life as a singer-songwriter was ruined before it even began. Because of who her mother was, she would never be taken seriously. And now, even in the massage chair, she couldn't relax. "They should call it Café Put Me Down."

"Babe, you can't think like that," Mac said, nibbling on her chocolate ice cream. Her face was caked in a baby blue mask, and she looked like a Smurf. "Think of it as a learning experience."

"Ugh," Coco groaned. "If this is learning, I prefer to remain undereducated."

"We knew this was not gonna be a cakewalk." Mac sighed and wiggled her freshly painted toenails. "If it were easy, it would be called *watching TV*. And really, who cares what a few coffee shop losers think anyway." Mac waved her hand dismissively.

"Those are the same losers I want to be my fans, remember?" Coco plopped her head against the plush chair and sighed. "It was like a room full of Finns."

Mac winced. "That scrufftastic kid gave you a complex."

"But he's right," Coco explained. "As long as I'm Coco Kingsley, no one is going to give me credit as an artist. " She sighed. "What I still can't figure out is how they recognized me. I mean, sure, I've been photographed with my mom before, but—"

"Well, now is probably not the best time to show you this, but you're going to see it eventually. . . ." Mac reached into her python-printed magazine tote and pulled out a copy of *Us Weekly*. She opened it to a middle page and handed it to Coco.

The headline read, CARDAMMON BACK AND BETTER THAN EVER! It was a piece about Cardammon's comeback

113

tour, complete with a photo spread of the gaudy outfits Cardammon was planning to wear in the show. Coco's eyes slid over to the sidebar: AND SHE'S BRINGING BABY C! The short piece talked about "rumors" that Coco would be appearing onstage with Cardammon during select shows. Above it was a photo montage of Coco through the years: the baby pictures that had appeared in *People*, the Halloween she and her mom both dressed as belly dancers, Coco stretching after taking a class at her father's hotel in Casablanca. Finally there was a picture of Coco leaving Karma Café, her guitar case slung over her shoulder.

"Oh no," Coco groaned.

"Oh yes, Baby C," Mac winked. "We need a plan. . . ."

Coco looked at her friend dubiously. The only thing scarier than having your baby pictures in *Us Weekly* was getting roped into one of Mac's crazy schemes.

"Right now you don't have a shot—you can't even get a song out." Mac waved the magazine excitedly. "All we need is for people to give you a chance *before* they realize you're Cardammon's daughter."

The woman painting Coco's toes suddenly stopped and looked up. "*You're* Cardammon's daughter?!" she squealed. "'Forever Blue' was my prom song! I *love* her!"

Coco shot Mac a *see?* glance. "My mother is inescapable."

But Mac was undeterred. "We'll make you unrecognizable. You're going to be Carda-*non*."

Coco crossed her arms vigilantly. Emily, the last victim of one of Mac's schemes, had been forced to walk around school for a week as a mountain-man freak named Spazmo. "I'm not ready for any of your makeovers."

"Make*under*," Mac corrected. "I want you to get the Ashlee Simpson look."

Coco tilted her head, thinking of Ashlee. "You want me to dye my hair red?"

"No, I mean early Ashlee, reality show Ashlee, black hair alterna-Ashlee," Mac explained. "We're going for the pre–nose job, pre-Pete, pre-blond version. She had to de-Jess herself, and that's exactly what we're going to do with you. We'll un-Card you and make you un-cute—not that you could ever not be cute," she added.

Coco considered the strategy. It *had* worked for Ashlee. . . . She felt her willpower escaping. "But how am I supposed to be *uncute* in a *kind of* cute way?"

Mac tilted her head toward the waiting room. There, in a colorful knit dress over a purple turtleneck, was Erin, bopping to her iPod. She looked like she had been dressed by an ancient Incan.

Mac smiled a devilish grin. "Just leave it to me."

chapter
Fourteen

emily

◀ Wednesday   September 30 ▶

7 PM   Leave Sony

8 PM   Meet a friend

10:30 PM   Home to Casa Armstrong

Much to Emily's surprise, Disneyland looked exactly like she had expected. It was crowded with tourists, cameras in hand and fanny packs securely at their middles. The only surprise was the parking lot, which seemed to stretch for miles. They never showed that in brochures.

Emily had convinced the union driver, Charlie, to take her to Disneyland for her secret date with Davey, since Erin was notoriously bad at keeping secrets. If Mac found out, she'd be furious—but what she didn't know wouldn't hurt her.

Now Emily walked toward the VIP entrance, which looked like a green phone booth with gold trim, and was tucked away from all the general admission lines. Davey had told her to meet him there, but she still felt like an imposter. She, Emily Mungler, from Cedartown, Iowa, was going to meet Davey Farris Woodward at the VIP booth at Disneyland, and she hadn't even won a radio contest. Her mind was spinning, wondering what he wanted to talk to her about. She imagined Davey asking her if she felt the same way about him. She'd look into his blue eyes and say *Yes, Davey. Oh, yes.*

Emily was about to send Davey a text to let him know where she was when she gasped.

Walking toward her, blond hair blowing, arms crossed, aviators on, was Mac. She looked like a drill sergeant.

"Nice try," Mac said as she stopped in front of Emily, wearing J Brand jeans and a tight striped cardigan. She crossed her tanned arms triumphantly.

"What are you doing here?" Emily hissed. She scoured the parking lot for signs of Davey, terrified he would see them talking and then invite Mac to hang out just to be polite. And then they would never be alone.

"Did you seriously think you were fooling me?" Mac asked. "You're here to 'meet a friend,'" she said, quoting Emily's iPhone schedule. "And since I know where Becks and Coco are, and it's definitely not in *Anaheim*. . . . Well, who else could you be meeting?"

Emily shook her head, flabbergasted. For a second she felt guilty for not telling Mac, but then she snapped out of it. She didn't have to tell Mac everything. Did she?

Before Emily could protest, Davey strolled toward them in Diesel jeans and a navy polo shirt. Seeing Mac, Davey smiled warmly and waved.

"Mac Attack!" Davey said. "Didn't know we'd have a third tonight."

"We don't," Emily said hastily, surprising even herself with her boldness. After all, if Emily could improvise on a movie set, in front of hundreds of cast and crew, then surely she could do it in front of just Davey and Mac? "Mac was just dropping off a script for me." She smiled coolly. "But we're all set now. Thanks so much, Mac."

Mac's jaw dropped and she stared at Emily, her eyes wide with shock.

"It's silly to leave now!" Davey protested. "After you drove all this way."

"Oh, but Mac knows we don't have an extra ticket," Emily insisted.

"No worries, I got a silver pass," Davey said, adorably enthusiastic. "Gets me in everywhere, plus three guests."

"Um, hello Davey! You're a movie star!" Mac raised her eyebrow. "Why did you buy a silver pass when you have a golden ticket? Your *face* will get you in anywhere."

"I don't want special treatment just because I'm famous." Davey shrugged. "I just want to be normal."

"Normal is not for people like us," Mac scolded, shaking her finger cutely at Davey.

Emily stared at Davey, expecting him to be annoyed by Mac's bossiness. But instead he was grinning.

"Well, we'll miss you!" Emily sighed, fake sadly. She took a step toward the entrance. "We should get going!"

"Aren't you coming, Mac?" Davey was practically begging.

"Listen *Dorkey Woodward*." Mac ran her fingers through her blond hair, which went all the way down her back. "I don't do lines."

"I bet you a pair of Mickey ears that we won't wait more than five minutes," he shot back, undeterred.

Mac tilted her head while she considered the offer. "Fiiiiine," she said finally, as though she were doing them a great favor by third-wheeling it. "But only for a little bit."

An hour later, Emily was experiencing levels of frustration she hadn't known were humanly possible. It should have been a thrilling time—everywhere they went, people seemed to do doubletakes when they saw Davey. First a look, then a whiplash headspin that seemed to say, *Did I just see Davey Woodward?* Emily wanted to be proud that she was with him, but being angry at Mac was taking up too much energy.

They reached Fantasyland, where Snow White and one of the dwarves stood in front of a tulip garden.

"So, what did you want to talk to me about?" Emily asked Davey quietly, when Mac was safely occupied checking a voice mail.

"Oh . . ." Davey glanced over at Mac. "Maybe it'd

be better if we talked later," he whispered. Emily felt a fresh wave of annoyance at Mac, but she was glad that Davey wanted to keep this quiet too. The way things were looking, they'd have to be sneaky if they wanted to get around Mac.

"What are we talking about?" Mac asked nosily as she ambled over, shutting off her phone.

"Um, we're going to take a picture!" Emily said quickly, pulling out her iPhone to snap a portrait of their group. "With Snow White and the dwarves!" she added, moving toward the tulip garden.

"Oh my God!" Snow White put her hands on her mouth when she spotted Davey, reaching for Dopey's gloved hand.

Dopey shook in his blue velvet pants and ripped off the dwarf head. Apparently, in real life, Dopey was an eighteen-year-old redheaded girl. Seeing Davey, she screamed at the top of her lungs.

"Easy now!" Davey put his hands up.

"WE LOVE YOU SO MUCH!" Snow White yelled. She didn't sound sweet or gentle, like Snow White. She sounded scary and obsessed.

Davey looked at Mac and Emily. "Follow me!"

With that, he took off, running through the park. They ran through Fantasyland, and Frontierland, and Critter Country—with Snow White and Dopey behind them, screaming, "Davey Woodward!" at the top of their lungs.

Soon other people had caught on to the Davey-chase. Panting and out of breath, Emily glanced behind her, and saw the Disney characters, plus a few cheerleaders in yellow-and-black uniforms tailing her like love-struck bumblebees. She just kept following Davey's navy polo shirt through the crowd. Soon he made a sharp right turn behind a little shack near Splash Mountain. He yanked Mac and Emily to his side and they all hid behind a green trash can.

"We're safe here!" he whispered. "Just wait for them to pass."

Emily clamped her mouth shut and waited while the girls stormed by. Sure enough, they didn't think to make the sharp right turn.

When the girls had passed, Mac reached into her Balenciaga bag and pulled out a blue bandana. "It's a good thing I always carry backup," she said, tying the cloth around Davey's head like he was Axl Rose. Then she slid her Ray-Bans over his eyes. "It's a disguise!"

Davey laughed and Emily felt her heart in her feet. Of course *Mac* was the one to save the day.

"You guys wait here, okay? I need to grab something else for my getup." He smiled and a tiny dimple next to his lips emerged.

When Davey was out of earshot, she turned to Mac. "Whatever happened to trusting your clients?" she hissed.

"Exsqueeze me?" Mac pretended to be shocked. "You were the one who lied to *moi*."

Emily bit her lip and focused her gaze on Mac's eyebrows—it was easier than looking her in the eyes—and steadied herself to tell Mac how she really felt.

"Listen," Mac cut in, her tone more serious now. "I'm doing this for *you*. It's like me and Pinkberry—sometimes the things you want most in life just aren't good for you."

Emily opened her mouth to protest, but before she could get a word out, Davey returned, smiling broadly, with a pair of mouse ears.

Mac looked at the ears suspiciously. "What are you doing with those?"

"I thought they'd be good for my disguise."

Suddenly Davey's expression turned serious as he looked at something behind them. "Guess some people see through this disguise."

Emily followed his gaze and spotted a man in a khaki-colored vest lurking by the line, snapping photos of Davey.

Emily couldn't help but smile. Maybe she'd wind up in pictures with Davey in *Us Weekly*. Then their relationship would be out in the national media, and there would be nothing Mac could do to stop *that*. Emily smiled her best *look at me I'm in love* smile, hoping the photographer would see her natural, happy glow, and know that this one was a front cover. *Young Hollywood's Newest It*

Couple! But every time the photographer inched closer, Mac leaned closer to Davey, blocking Emily with her body. The photographer took a giant step closer, as if to take one last shot.

As Emily stepped closer to Davey, she realized the flashes had already gone off, and the photographer had gotten his shot. Emily knew he hadn't captured the first image of SkyWard—instead, it was of *MacWood*.

Emily was too flustered even to fake-smile. Mackenzie Little-Armstrong—her supposed BFF, her agent, and now her *babysitter*—was officially ruining everything.

chapter
FIFTeen

mac

◄ Thursday October 1 ►

5 AM Early breakfast

6 AM Finish reading Josh Schwartz script
for E

8 AM Research sponsorship opportunities
for B

9 AM Tutoring (3 hours)

Sometime today: MNMD

Reminder: TAKE CHARGE!

Mac stood in Emily's hair and makeup trailer, staring at the circus surrounding her starlet. Lisette the manicurist was filing her nails, Theadora the costume designer was holding shirts up to Emily's face, Tina was misting Emily's forehead with Evian, and Robyn was applying a sticky gel to the ends of her hair. The tall PA was scribbling Emily's M Café de Chaya order on pages of an old script.

"Wonder what Shane's psychic said today?" Tina mused to the group.

Everyone laughed loudly, even Emily. Mac didn't understand what was so hilarious—especially when Emily hadn't said more than *hello* to her since Disneyland. Everything she did was for the good of Team Emily—including MNMD: Mission No More Davey. She was going to tell him, as soon as possible, that being together was *not* an option. She'd been weak, flirting with him at Disneyland, and now she had to be strong, for the good of Emily, their friendship, and both of their careers. Unfortunately, Emily would never know about Mac's sacrifice or be able to thank her for it. And there was nothing Mac hated more than not getting credit where credit was due.

Mac was even crabbier because between Becks, Coco, and Emily, her phone was ringing nonstop. She was beginning to feel like she needed an assistant just to take calls. And then, as if on cue, Mac's phone rang again.

"Hey Becksie! What's up?" Mac chirped, channeling her inner Adrienne.

The trailer was silent, and Emily shot Mac a stern look. "Can you take that outside?"

Diva much? Mac thought to herself, but she rolled her eyes and decided it was a good moment to get breakfast anyway. At least that way she and Emily could have some space. Without a word, Mac sauntered out of the trailer, letting the door slam behind her.

"So I still don't know what to wear to the photo shoot tomorrow," Becks whined, as Mac walked toward the catering tent. "They don't use stylists 'cause they want it to be authentic—"

"*Authentic* is just another word for *ugly*," Mac interrupted, spooning fresh blueberries onto her plain Greek yogurt and stack of cinnamon challah French toast. "You do know that, right?"

"Um . . ." Becks paused. "No?"

Ordinarily Mac would have been happy to debate

the semantics of *authentic* versus *ugly* but she had just spotted Davey Woodward coming toward her. She knew that she could fix Becks's authenticity issues with a phone call, but what she had to take care of in person, right that second, was Davey.

"Don't worry, I'm on it," Mac said. "Ciao bella!" Without waiting for her friend's reply, Mac ended the call and tucked the phone into her pocket.

Davey stood in front of her, his thumbs tucked into his Diesel jeans. "Hey, check this out." He pulled out his iPhone to show Mac a picture he'd taken of them on Big Thunder Railroad at Disneyland. It was actually a really cute shot—they were leaning into each other, Davey's mouth wide open in an excited yell, Mac's head thrown back in exhilaration.

Mac forced herself to smile coolly and took a seat at the picnic tables where the PAs ate. Normally Mac did not eat with the crew, and as a personal rule she did not eat in front of boys, but she had no choice. She had to have this conversation now, as far away from Emily as possible.

Davey trailed along, exactly as Mac had expected. "You know, we never finished our conversation the other day. I was hoping we could talk—you know, about what I said. . . ."

Mac covered her half-full mouth. "Why?" But what she really meant was, *Why* did he have to make things so difficult?

Davey laughed. "Just my luck that every girl in America loves me, and I can't even get you to notice me."

Mac sighed. Nothing could be further from the truth. She didn't just *notice* him. She noticed when he rotated his polo shirts from Ben Sherman to Ralph. When he wore the Rolex instead of the Patek Philippe. When he left a few strands of hair sticking up or slicked them down.

"Listen . . . if you want me to leave you alone. . . ." Davey trailed off. His eyebrows were knit in concern, but there was a glimmer of hope in his eyes. "*Do* you want me to leave you alone?"

Mac shook her head miserably. She reminded herself that if they were to ever get together, Emily would crumple like a paper doll. And then it would be *adieu*, Emily the star and Mac the A-list agent, and *adieu* to their friendship, and hello, lame old life. And no boy—not even Davey Woodward—was worth *that*.

Mac's heart pounded in her Stella McCartney T-shirt. She thought of that guy in *A Tale of Two Cities*, a book that had been on the BAMS summer reading list, who gave up his own life for the good of his love. She told herself she was making a great sacrifice for the sake of her friend, and felt a little stronger. "Davey, I'm sorry if you got the wrong idea, but—"

And then, before Mac could stop him, he grabbed her hand. "I'm serious, Mac! What does a guy have to do to get you?"

Her stomach twisted into a knot. One decibel louder and there would be no saving Emily. Tawker would be all over this in a second. She racked her brain for ways to make it stop, but she'd already tried everything: denial, avoidance, politeness, and rudeness—and nothing worked. There was only one option left. One very risky, very unattractive option: telling the truth.

Mac squeezed Davey's hand to quiet him. Electricity shot through her, and she took her hand away. "Listen. This is super awkward for me." She winced, knowing she was about to betray a confidence, but she reminded herself she was doing this *for* her friend. "The thing is, Emily really . . . she kind of has a thing for you—"

Davey shook his head. "Emily's great but she's not my type. I was only hanging out with her to find out how to get to *you*. *You're* my type, Mac. It's always been—"

"DAVEY!" Mac practically screamed. She was about to say, *There will never ever be anything between us*, but before she could get the words out, she spotted Kimmie Tachman, walking past their table, clutching her iBook. She was staring at Mac and Davey, a fascinated smile on her face, a delighted twinkle in her brown eyes.

Mac raised her voice to be sure that Kimmie heard what she was about to say. "Sorry, Emily is too busy to star in another movie with you."

"Wha?" Davey jerked back, looking confused and hurt. "Did you even hear what I said?"

Mac stood up and dropped her half-eaten French toast into a wire trash can.

"Yes, and Emily's schedule is full. Thanks anyway!" Mac charged out of the tent so fast that she almost knocked into Kimmie. "Ohheysweetsdidn'tseeyou therebye!"

She marched forcefully back to Emily's trailer, her Tory Burch flats slapping loudly on the hot pavement. But before she stepped inside, she allowed herself one look back at Davey.

He was still sitting at the picnic table, a sad hangdog look on his face. It seemed MNMD was a success. She should be proud of herself.

But she didn't feel satisfied at all.

chapter
sixteen

coco

◀ Thursday   October 1 ▶

3 PM   Tell Cardamommy I can't do reunion tour

3:30 PM   Makeunder shopping spree extravaganza begins!

5 PM   Sneak preview of New Coco in dance studio

9 PM   Café de Chaya, anyone?

Thursday after school, Coco marched toward her dance studio, the offending *Us Weekly* tucked under her arm. She found Cardammon wearing a sparkly green leotard and matching boa, doing a revamped version of the Flame in the mirror, waving her arms like a crazy woman. It didn't look retro-chic—it looked mega-lame.

Coco grabbed the remote control and zapped the Bose speakers in the corner of the ceiling, abruptly shutting off the music. There was only the sound of the eco-friendly air-conditioner in the studio.

"Mom," Coco said. She hoisted the *Us Weekly* article at her mother. "I told you, I don't want to do this."

Cardammon wiped a trickle of sweat off her brow with a green armband. She eyed the article, then appraised her daughter. "Sorry, luv. We'd already released the photos before our chat."

Coco crossed her arms over her chest to show her

mom she was serious, expecting a fight. "Well, I'm not doing it."

"I see. . . ." Cardammon looked around at the sea of sequins and feather boas. "It's not the outfits, is it?" She ran a bright green fingernail over a glittery, sexy Little Red Riding Hood outfit. "They *are* a little over the top. I hope I'm not about to make a giant arse of myself." She sighed and looked at Coco. "I'm *not*, right?"

Coco froze. She hadn't expected this to become a *dialogue*. And while the outfits were problematic, they weren't what was making her want to run from the reunion tour.

"Or is it the dancing? I was afraid it was a little dated. . . ." She trailed off. "Or the songs? They're all wrong, aren't they?" she asked, her eyes getting surprisingly misty.

Coco stared at her mother in shock, her heart aching. She wasn't used to seeing Cardammon anything but blithe and blissfully unaware, and her sudden vulnerability shook Coco like an 8.5 earthquake. She didn't know what to think, let alone say. *Yes, your outfits are tackier than Cher in Vegas? You're too old to be dancing like a stripper? Your music was* always *embarrassing?*

"I just . . ." Cardammon wiped her nose against the back of her hand. "I thought you would want to do this with me, but . . . maybe I'm just an embarrassment now," she finished, almost to herself.

Coco would have said almost anything to make her

mom feel better. Anything but the one thing she wanted to hear. She took a deep breath. "The tour's going to be great," Coco lied. "My decision's got nothing to do with you, Mom."

Cardammon's eyebrows arched hopefully. "Really?"

"Really," Coco told her earnestly. "It's me. I'm done with singing."

Almost instantly, Cardammon looked like herself again. Her shoulders snapped back and with one swipe under her eyes, she was back to normal. "Well, you're old enough to make your own decisions about these things." She gave Coco a light peck on the forehead.

Coco smiled encouragingly. Sure it was a white lie. But it was a lot kinder than the truth.

A few hours later, Mac, Coco, and Erin stood in Coco's private dance studio, preparing to see Coco's new look. Cardammon was meeting with her life coach, who lived in Palm Springs, so they were safe for at least three hours.

They had just returned from their MCM: Mission Coco Makeunder shopping spree, which began at Whole Foods and ended at a used clothing store called Wasteland. Coco had traded in a Marc Jacobs smock from his 2008 collection to buy a tan pleather vest, three dresses, big tan cowboy boots, red plastic sunglasses, and a black velvet beret.

They'd bought all of Erin's must-haves: mineral-based lipstick, plum-colored eyeliner, and purple eye shadow, all of which Erin had expertly applied. Then Mac forced Coco to put the clothes on in the bathroom— with the lights off.

"Say hello to the artist formerly known as Coco Kingsley," Mac joked, turning Coco toward the mirror.

Coco's jaw dropped as she saw her reflection. She barely recognized herself. She wore a royal blue halter dress that tied around her neck and went all the way down to her cowboy boots. Erin's peacock feather earrings tickled her cheeks and her tastefully subtle highlights were now tinted pink thanks to a heavy dose of Crystal Light.

Erin beamed approvingly at Coco's new look. "You look mad cool. Capital *M*, capital *A*, capital *D*." Normally an outfit compliment from Erin would have made Coco want to change *immédiatement*, but she reminded herself that today this was a *good* thing.

"Just in case you forgot how to spell *mad*," Mac teased. She turned to Coco. "Isn't it nice to know that you can rock both Versace and vintage?"

"No offense, but this is *not* vintage," Coco insisted, touching the polyester. The dress smelled like car garage. "This is OPG." Coco cringed. "Other People's Germs."

"It's more like Other People's *Gems*," Erin insisted.

Coco pivoted her body to examine herself in the mirror. Then she smiled: *Mission accomplished*. But there was one other thing. . . .

"From now on"—Coco paused for dramatic effect—"I'm *Cordelia Rose*."

She'd come up with the idea this afternoon, in the middle of writing her new song *A Name Ain't Nothing but Letters*. Suddenly it hit her: The only thing better than not *looking* like Cardammon's daughter was not *being* Cardammon's daughter. *No name, no shame.* Besides, she'd told her mom she was done with singing, and now it was true: Coco Kingsley was done with singing. Cordelia Rose was just getting started. And Cardammon didn't need to know a thing about it.

"Cordelia *what*?" Mac made a face like she'd been force-fed supermarket sushi. "You don't need a new name. You have a great name. A famous name. You do want to be famous, don't you?" Mac asked her, although it was more of a statement than a question.

Erin looked back and forth between Coco and Mac like she was watching Wimbledon. She cleared her throat and cleaned her glasses on her Irish wool sweater. "Yeah, I have to go with Mac on this one. What's cuter than Coco K.? Nothing."

Coco tapped her cowboy boot impatiently. "Don't you get it? No name, no shame?"

"Babe, no." Mac said firmly. "*No name, no fame* is more like it. Ashlee Simpson didn't go around calling herself Ashlee Daisy." Mac twirled her wooden Mintee bracelet. "She wanted to *differentiate* herself from Jess, not disown her."

"And the Jonas Brothers all have the same last name," Erin added emphatically. "*Jonas*."

Mac looked at Coco seriously. "You already have fame, and fame is like currency. You gotta be smart about how you spend it. You don't just chuck it like that!" She snapped her fingers.

Coco closed her eyes and took a deep breath. She wondered if she and Mac were just naturally too far apart on this one. Sure, Mac's mother was known in Hollywood circles, but Coco's mother was famous *around the world*. Mac did not know what it was like to show up for Halloween every year and see half the girls in your class dressed as your mother. Mac never had to hold a book at a forty-five-degree angle to hide from paparazzi. Coco shook her head. "I love you, Mac Little-A, but I *have* to do this. I need to know they hate me—or love me—because of who I am, not because of who my mother is."

Coco—make that Cordelia Rose—stared at herself in the mirror. She was ready to find out if she had talent, once and for all.

CHAPTER seventeen

mac

◀ Thursday   October 1 ▶

3 PM   Mission Coco Makeunder

5 PM   Back to set

6:30 PM Dinner with Mama A @ The Hump

Reminder: TAKE CHARGE!

Mac sat at a sleek table at The Hump restaurant in Santa Monica, across from her mother. Located atop the tarmac of the Santa Monica airport, overlooking the private jets and the Pacific Ocean, it was the best view in all of Los Angeles County. Adrienne liked to take Mac there, because she thought watching the planes take off was a reminder of endless possibility. Plus she loved their hamachi. Normally Mac was inspired by the view, but that day she felt confused and drained as she took a bite of her edamame.

She waited for her mother's head to pop up from her BlackBerry. It was Mac's first full week of being an agent, and she had more questions than a newbie watching *Lost*.

"Ciao for now darling," Adrienne said into her phone. Then she hit a button and tossed her BlackBerry into her Birkin bag like it was a cheap toy. It was a signal that, at least, for now, Mac had her mother's full attention. Adrienne tweaked her rectangular Armani glasses straight across her nose and swooshed her reddish-brown bob to face Mac. She was ready.

"So give me an update. How are things?" Adrienne asked. She turned her call sheet over so she would be less tempted to look at the long list of people whose phone calls she had to return.

"Everything seems to be going well," Mac said carefully. She didn't want to tell her mom about the tension with Emily, the fact that Becks was needier than a newborn bird, or that Coco seemed to be in the middle of a full-on identity crisis. And she especially didn't want to get into her Daveydrama. Because, Mac told herself, there *was* no drama. It was over. Fini. She'd taken care of it. Though as Mac stared out at the endless blue of the Pacific Ocean, she just felt . . . sad. "But I have my doubts," she added as she took a sip of her miso soup.

Adrienne sighed. "Of course you do. You're a woman. We're always doubting ourselves. Terrible habit."

"It's not just that," Mac said quickly. She knew her mother's *women doubt themselves too much* speech by heart.

Mac looked down at the last remains of her nails, which were chewed down to the cuticles. Between being a life coach, career advisor, stylist, and shrink to her friends, she hadn't had time for a manicure.

Mac knew she couldn't keep living like this. It was barbaric. "How do I know if I'm really cut out to be an agent?"

"What do you mean, *how*?" Adrienne looked at Mac impatiently. Adrienne firmly believed that there *were* stupid questions. "Either you get great joy from seeing them succeed—and you treat their success as your own—or you find something else to do." Adrienne took a bite of her yellowtail hamachi. She closed her eyes blissfully.

"Most of what we do is cheerleading," Adrienne added. "You have to love cheering your clients on, making their dreams come true. There is no greater reward than that in this business."

Mac thought of Emily, and how all she really wanted was Davey. Sure, she wanted to be an actress too, but Davey was her real dream. And Emily was Mac's client. So technically, Mac was supposed to want Emily to end up with Davey . . . except that she *didn't*. It was hard enough to see them act together on a movie set, but to imagine them together in real life? No way. But maybe, Mac thought, she would in time?

"Are you making your clients happy, kitten?" Adrienne asked.

Mac thought of Becks being flustered by a little thing like beach accessories, Coco changing her name, Emily spewing mints on Davey. "I'm not so sure I am," she admitted.

Adrienne tilted her head to the side, thinking. "If your friends are feeling down, give them something to feel good about." She straightened her glasses and stared at Mac. "Moping like this isn't going to help anyone."

Mac tapped her ragged fingers on the table as she tried to think of what would make them happy. These days, she had no time for shopping or slumber parties or advance movie screenings or brunch at La Conversation or any of the Inner Circle's usual standbys. The only block of free time she had was Saturday night—which gave her an idea.

"Hey Mom," Mac said, sweetly. "Could I have a party at our house? On Saturday? To celebrate how everyone is doing?"

Adrienne paused to consider the idea. Adrienne never said anything unless she meant it; it was a good sign that she hadn't yet said *no*. But she hadn't said yes yet, either. Mac tried not to cringe, waiting for the answer.

She pointed her chopstick at Mac. "Okay, but one caveat: Don't spread yourself too thin, Mackenzie. Remember our deal. Your word is—"

"—your honor," Mac finished obediently.

"And you have given me your word that you will get good grades, keep up your family obligations, and generally not become as crazy as everyone else in this business," Adrienne reminded her.

Mac smiled—that was simple. Hollywood was so bananas, it was easy to look sane. She took a last slurp of her miso soup and noticed that it tasted good again.

To: Inner Circle
From: Mac
Subject: Save the date! October 3! Star Power Party!
FOR YOU!

Ladies of the Inner Circle!

Get ready, because I'm throwing a party in your honor at my house this Saturday, to celebrate you and your star power. We're talking paparazzi, red carpets, and your beautiful selves—can you say *debut*?

Deets to follow.

Love,
Mac

CHapter
EIGHTEEN

becks

◀ Friday   October 2 ▶

3:30 PM   Afternoon surf session

6 PM   Choose accessories for shoot tomorrow

7 PM   Dinner @ CPK

B ecks and her father stood nervously in the middle of her bedroom. It was a clear day, and they could see Steven Spielberg's compound down the beach, and Dustin Hoffman and his wife walking their Labradors. At that moment, however, Clutch and Becks weren't admiring the Malibu scenery. They were staring at Becks's closet, their heads tilted to the side, their jaws slightly open.

They were stumped.

Their mission was to select accessories for Becks's photo shoot the next day, since the Dixie Gals were all self-styled. They'd been at it for ten minutes, and so far Clutch had said nothing for nine of them. Even though it seemed like a simple decision, Becks knew she *couldn't* fail. If she picked something stupid, she'd be disappointing the Dixie Gals, Mac, and herself.

"Havin' fun yet, Pops?" Becks joked.

Clutch Becks was famous for his death-defying

stunts, like running across fire, but he looked terrified in the face of fashion. Just like his daughter.

Becks grabbed some large turquoise bracelets made of plastic. They had been her favorites in sixth grade, but now she was pretty sure they were completely LY. She held them up for her father to judge.

Clutch looked quizzically at the bracelets. "Maybe, but. . . ." He didn't finish his sentence. Instead he twirled his hair with his index finger.

"You have good taste, Becksy," Clutch insisted. "What do you like?"

Becks shook her head. Trusting herself was *not* an option. Not for something so important. She pulled out her phone again to text Mac for advice, but then put it away. She'd already sent three SOS messages with no response. It was beginning to feel like Mac was ignoring her. She really needed her best friend—not to mention her agent—right now. She still didn't know what had happened to the last fourth Dixie Gal, and she didn't want to make a terrible mistake.

"Don't worry if you don't know," Becks assured her father. "Just go with your instincts and say *yay* or *nay*. Starting with this." She reached for a leather bracelet that she'd bought in Hawaii.

"Kiddo, I *really* don't know about these things. Look at me!" Clutch waved at himself. He was wearing his uniform: Dockers shorts, a Tommy Bahama button-up, and green Crocs. "My answer to every fashion question is green Crocs."

Becks knew her father was right. But she'd already tried Emily, who was completely caught up in learning her script, and Coco, whose style overhaul had rendered her useless, too. She'd tried asking the Dixie Gals at Sloopy's, but that hadn't worked either.

"It's times like these I really wish. . . ." Clutch didn't say what they were both thinking, which was that it would be so much easier if Becks's mother were around. She had died when Becks was just a baby, and for as long as Becks could remember, it had just been her and Clutch. Most times, they did fine on their own. But there were other times, like now, when having a mother would have made life so much easier. Beck sighed, sadness washing over her.

"I just don't want to steer you wrong," Clutch said finally. "Can't you call one of the girls? Isn't Mac good at this stuff?"

"Yes, but. . . ." Mac had said she'd take care of it, but it was the night before the shoot, and so far nothing. Besides, Mac was busy getting everything ready for their big party tomorrow night, and Becks didn't want to bother her. She also didn't want to get into the drama of it all with her father, who was about as helpful when it came to girl politics as he was with accessory selection. "You're all I got, Pops," Becks said. She was surprised at how alone she sounded.

Just then the doorbell rang.

Clutch and Becks darted downstairs to discover a girl who looked about eighteen, with pink hair in a pixie haircut wearing a polka-dot top with silver ballet flats. "Special delivery from Xochi," the girl said, hoisting three giant shopping bags toward Becks.

Becks smiled. Xochi (pronounced "Zo-hee") Dawn was Mac's personal stylist, the woman who dressed starlets for their paparazzi opps. So Mac really was on top of this!

As Becks closed the door, she opened the gold-embossed envelope that was stapled to one of the bags and pulled out a cream-colored card.

HI GIRL! MAC SAID YOU WOULD NEED THESE FOR THE
SHOOT TOMORROW. THESE BATHING SUITS WILL BE PERF.

Becks couldn't believe she'd doubted Mac! Until she read the rest of the letter.

JUST BE CAREFUL—THEY'RE DELICATE—AND ABSOLUTELY
DON'T GET THEM WET. XOXO, XOCHI

Becks dropped the heavy card back into one of the bags. *Don't get a bathing suit wet?* That was like giving someone a Sprinkles cupcake and telling them not to eat it. Becks peered inside the bag and noticed a black tankini with gold charms. It would have been perfect for

Vogue, but it was totally useless to Becks. The next suit was tinted green and made out of a thin fabric that felt like rice paper. The rest of the stash was more swimsuits, and Becks didn't even bother to look through them. Mac obviously hadn't been listening when she'd explained that she needed *accessories*, not swimsuits.

"Well these are interesting," Clutch said hopefully, but he was back to twirling his hair, never a good sign.

Becks shook her head. Mac might have known about Hollywood—but Becks was beginning to wonder if Mac really knew about *her*.

Dear Mac,

It was great to meet you at Urth for the Star Power planning meeting. It will be a magical event! Your guests will heart the red-carpet themes.

Also had a follow-up question per our last convo. Did you want *real* paparazzi or faux? With faux we can control what pictures they take and send them ourselves to the photo wires. Just a thought. Please get back to me at your earliest convenience.

Cheers,
Elena

To: Elena K. @ Elena K. Events
From: Mackenzie Little-Armstrong
Subject: Re: Party/real paparazzi or faux

Elena,

Great meeting you, too. I'm psyched about the themes and menus.

As for your other question: I don't do fake anything.

XO
MLA

emily

◀ Friday   October 2 ▶

6 PM   iChat Paige

6:30 PM   Go through sides for tonight's shoot

8 PM   Night shoot begins!

Emily lay on her white Duxiana comforter in the guest bedroom of the Armstrong house. She was dressed in her navy Harajuku Lovers pajamas (a start gift from the casting agent), trying to rest because she had a night shoot later that evening. Emily grabbed a handful of cheddar Chex Mix and crunched loudly. Paige had mailed her a care package of Chex Mix and apple Fig Newtons, since the Armstrongs had no junk food in their house and ate organic everything. Sometimes Emily just needed to eat like a normal person.

The Armstrongs were at a family dinner at some Italian restaurant, which was supposedly the best in Beverly Hills—but to Emily, pasta was pasta. Of course, Emily had been invited, but she had pretended that she needed to run lines. She didn't want to intrude, but mostly she needed a break from Mac. She plopped her laptop onto a white satin pillow so she could iChat with Paige.

Even though the Armstrongs made sure Emily felt at home, she still felt out-of-place in her room. It was called "the Gift Closet," because it was where the Armstrongs kept wacky gifts that they didn't want to toss or keep on display. It was like a Museum of Celebrity Bad Taste, Emily thought, scanning the walls. There was a signed *Sea Devils* poster (from Davey Woodward—*sigh* . . .), a statue of a ballerina (a new addition from Christina Aguilera), and an old brass owl (an inside joke, apparently, from Owen Wilson) stared down at her from the wall.

Finally Paige's face popped onto the computer screen. Paige had small Renée Zellweger eyes and big chipmunk cheeks. She had brown hair, which she'd parted into three ponytails: two on the side and one on top of her head. Sometimes Emily was afraid that Paige was going to be one of those people who got *really* weird in high school. But for now, she was the most loyal friend a girl could ask for.

"Hold on one sec," Emily whispered, paranoia-checking herself. She ran over and locked the door, just in case Mac came home early and barged in. When she returned to her computer screen, she whispered, "Mac is driving me crazy." Normally Emily hated to complain, because she was super-grateful that Mac had discovered her. But right now, she had to vent. "She crashed my date with Davey!"

"That's ridonkulous!" Paige snorted. After Mac had

deemed Paige Not Cool Enough when they met, Paige had decided she was Not A Fan. "Why? I mean, what's wrong with her?"

"Well, there's a little more to the story," Emily admitted. "Remember how I freaked out on the first day?"

Paige nodded and her three ponytails bounced. "You ate the tuna sandwich." She remembered everything so well that sometimes it felt like she was Emily's diary.

"So Mac kinda made this rule so that I don't lose my job over Davey."

Paige shot Emily an *are you crazy?* look. "What kind of rule?"

"She decided she basically has to be my babysitter," Emily said. And then she launched into an explanation of the Disneyland hijacking. "She just showed up. Plus, whenever I try to have lunch to be near Davey, she insists on getting me food and bringing it to my trailer. And she's on set twenty-four seven. She's *always* there. It almost feels like she's stalking me."

Paige's brown eyes widened. She leaned into her computer so that her face looked like a giant bubble on Emily's screen. "Look," Paige said, crossing her arms. "Your agent is supposed to get you jobs, not systematically destroy your love life. And P.S., Mac needs you more than you need her. Without you she has nothing."

Emily winced. She didn't like to think that way. It seemed very diva-esque, and besides, she *only* had Hollywood opportunities *because* of Mac. "But she only has my best interests in mind. And if I have to choose between Davey and acting—"

"Remind me again," Paige interrupted. "How is being in love with Davey hurting your work? Aren't you supposed to fall in love with him in the movie?"

Emily toyed with a shiny blue button on her pajama top and looked into her best friend's digital eyes. "Yes, but so what?"

"Mac has done a mind job on you. You think it's *either* Davey *or* acting. But really, you *can* have it all." Paige pumped her fists like a football coach. "You gotta *use* that love for Davey in every scene. Because the only thing better than acting is the real thing."

Emily thought back to all the times she'd willed tears to get her way or even feigned happiness over bad gifts. As good an actress as she was—and she was, even if that sounded a little conceited to admit—she was never as convincing as when she *actually* cried or was *actually* grateful. Maybe *actually* being in love with Davey was the best thing that ever happened to her.

"You know what?" Emily said, feeling her mood lifting like steam in the shower. "I think you may be a genius." And then she did a little fist-pump right back at her oldest—and *best*—friend.

CHAPTER
TWENTY

mac

◀ Friday   October 2 ▶

8 PM   Family Dinner at Il Pastaio

10 PM   Jet to set

Reminder: TAKE CHARGE!

Mac dipped her focaccia into the last of the pasta sauce on her plate. She and her family were at Il Pastaio, a place she normally loved, but right now all she wanted was for dinner to be over. She had a million things to do—including planning an A-list party—and her parents had an annoying habit of stretching dinners into three-hour ordeals so they could pretend to be chic and European. But tonight, a long dinner meant she might not make it back to set. Which meant that Davey and Emily could do who-knew-what without her. Which technically was for the best, but somehow still felt like the worst. A vision of the two costars kissing popped into her brain, and she let out a shuddering sigh. She felt more rattled than when she'd found out that Pinkberry contained no probiotics, and therefore could not be considered frozen yogurt at all.

Just then Mac's phone blared. Instantly the hope

that it might be Davey shot through her. Maybe he'd tell her that he'd thought about what she'd said but wasn't going to take no for an answer. Mac yanked her phone out of her purse, but her heart sank when she saw that it was Elena Kiriades, who was coordinating the Star Power party. The party was in less than twenty-four hours, which meant this might be a fiesta emergency. She looked pleadingly at her mom, to see if she might—just this once—be allowed to take a call at dinner.

Adrienne shook her head. It wasn't up for discussion.

Mac sighed, and obediently ignored the call.

"Would you mind if I told you about what I learned reading my online encyclopedia?" Mac's sister, Maude, asked politely. She had tiny golden curls and big eyes like Shiloh Jolie-Pitt. If Maude hadn't been her sister, Mac would have hated her for being so perfect.

Lanyard and Adrienne looked at each other and beamed. Their six-year-old genius was adorable *and* thoughtful. "Sure, honey," Adrienne said.

"Well, what a lot of people don't know about sharks"—Maude's eyes widened—"is that both their upper and lower jaws move."

Her sister hogging the spotlight offered Mac the perfect opportunity to discreetly check her voice mail. Turning her ear away from the table, Mac listened to the message: Apparently it was impossible to shut down a residential street for a red-carpet party and so did they want to put the red carpet in the backyard? Mac rolled her eyes. She'd explained this when she'd responded to the e-mail asking the same thing. Mac couldn't stand answering the same question twice. She slid her hands and phone onto her lap and sent Elena a sneaky text reply: NO BACKYARDS THIS ISN'T A JULY 4TH BBQ PLS FIGURE IT OUT!!! She sighed in frustration. Did she really have to tell *everyone* how to do their job?

The waiter approached to clear their plates, and Lanyard smiled at the waiter. "Could we take a look at the dessert menu?"

"Um, we've had three courses already. And Italian food isn't exactly *light*," Mac pointed out, hoping to play on her mother's caloric awareness. Adrienne wasn't as crazy as the Pilates-toned stay-at-home moms—but this was still L.A.

"Mac, don't talk to your father like that," Adrienne shot sternly. "I'll just have an espresso," she said politely to the waiter, handing him her empty dinner plate. "But please bring dessert menus for everyone else." The waiter nodded and walked off.

Mac sighed and leaned back in her chair, hoping that by being quiet she would not prolong this dinner any further.

Just then, her phone rang again. Becks.

"No, Mac," Adrienne said sternly.

Mac nodded at her mom to show that she knew the

rule, but gave her parents a pleading look. "Becks has a shoot tomorrow—what if she needs me?"

Lanyard looked at Mac sternly. "Call Becks *after*," he said, like it was some great solution Mac hadn't considered.

Mac moaned, staring at the phone in her lap that she was forbidden to use. "It's just that we've been here for hours."

"Are we keeping you from more important things?" Lanyard said.

Um, yes?

Before Mac could explain, Adrienne's BlackBerry blared its alarm-sound ring, which the entire Armstrong family knew meant that Davey Woodward was calling. All eyes zoomed in on Adrienne, wondering how she would play this in light of her recent phones-off-at-dinner discourse. Even Lanyard looked fascinated.

"Aren't you gonna get that?" Mac hissed. Maybe Davey was trying to reach *her*. Maybe if her mother picked up right now, Davey would be talking on the phone and therefore not be able to kiss Emily. No way could he call his agent and kiss someone at the same time. "It's *Davey*!" Mac practically yelled.

Adrienne stared at her daughter in shock. It was the kind of overly calm gaze Adrienne only gave before a storm.

"My darling daughter"—Adrienne spoke slowly in a voice that meant business—"I think what you need tonight is some sleep." She hit *ignore* on her BlackBerry, and Mac sat back, shocked.

"Mom, I'm not tired, I'm busy—"

"No. You have been acting like a very stressed-out girl. And it's because you're tired. Which is why," Adrienne calmly continued, "you're not allowed to use your cell phone or a computer or your iChat. Consider yourself in the Stone Age for the next twenty-four hours."

"But—" But she couldn't even finish her sentence. She was too busy calculating all the calls she would miss. The party plans that needed finalizing. How would she get through to Becks, Coco, and Emily? There would be no way to convey that she was out of commission.

"You're grounded," Adrienne finished, as if that wasn't already obvious.

"But Mom," Mac cried, "This is so unfair! All I did was make a few phone calls. That's *nothing*. You've never grounded me for anything that small." It was true: Just last month Mac had broken into her mom's office and called the *Deal With It* producers, pretending to be her mom, to get Emily an audition. Adrienne hadn't been pleased when she found out, but she also hadn't *grounded* Mac.

"Well," Adrienne said with a smug look on her face, "consider yourself grounded for all the worse things you've done before this." Before Mac could protest, her mom went on. "You can have the party tomorrow because your friends are counting on it. But from now on, agenting cannot interfere with your grades *or* your family."

Mac clutched the napkin on her lap. *But apparently her family could interfere with her agenting.*

Her brother, Jenner, snickered, and Maude just looked sad.

"'In the long run, men hit only what they aim at,'" Maude announced. "'Therefore, though they should fail immediately, they had better aim at something high.'"

Mac stared at her sister like she was an alien.

"Did you just quote Thoreau?" Lanyard asked, beaming at Maude in proud surprise.

Maude nodded.

"How did you know about him, honey?"

"Yesterday I was reading Gandhi and saw that he was inspired by Thoreau. . . ."

Mac stopped listening, her stomach aching with worry. She had a colossal party to plan, Becks was in need of fashion guidance, Coco *Rose* had been MIA all day, and Davey and Emily were probably off having way too much fun without her. She chewed her fingernail, wondering what Thoreau would have to say about *that*.

CHAPTER
TWENTY-ONE

emily

◀ Friday   October 2 ▶

8 PM Driver to take Emily to set

9 PM Night shoot

Emily walked slowly behind Chris on the Sony lot, smiling in the dark, cool L.A. night. He wore his usual uniform of corduroys, pumas, and a brown hoodie. That day's T-shirt said ALEXANDER PAYNE'S ABOUT SCHMIDT.

"So I looked up Truffaut," Emily told him. Chris had mentioned the director yesterday. Truffaut was his idol, since he'd left school as a teenager to start working on movies, too.

"You're failing me, Iowa," Chris said, shaking his head. "You're supposed to be a huge brat by now, and instead you're actually paying attention to me. Your friend—I mean, *agent*, on the other hand. . . ."

Emily smiled and decided that no comment was the best comment. A tiny part of her was glad she wasn't the only one who thought Mac could be difficult. Plus, she felt too inspired by her iChat with Paige to dwell on Mac's shortcomings. She *could* have it all: She could love Davey *and* be a great actress. Even better—the only person standing in her way was still at dinner.

That evening the *Deal With It* soundstage felt like a ghost town. The only people from production were Emily, Davey, Shane, and a few crew members to handle lights and sound. There weren't even any extras because the scene was supposed to be a private moment between Emily and Davey's characters in the computer lab.

The classroom set was bare, except for a giant poster of Niagara Falls on the back wall and three rows of empty desks, each with its own computer. Someone from the art department had written computer code on the chalkboard. Davey was waiting for her by one of the workstations. He sat in a swivel chair wearing a gray sweater dress, and his brunette wig was done in a chiffon knot. Spotting his costar, he spun around in a circle in his chair. Emily's heart pinged.

Shane stood next to Davey, doing yoga poses. At the moment, he was in Tree. "So listen up, dollface." He stepped out of the pose. "I looked up *gorgeous* in the dictionary and there's just a picture of you." He pointed both fingers at Emily.

Emily wanted to hug Shane for complimenting her in front of Davey. She hoped Davey was paying attention and that he'd noticed her Marc by Marc Jacobs heart leaf–print dress, and her faint scent of Vera Wang Princess.

Suddenly Shane closed his eyes and shook his head

quickly. "Yada yada yada! Less talking, more directing!" He looked right at Emily. "Do you know your lines?"

Emily nodded.

"Well, it doesn't matter, because we're just going to improvise this scene. I know I wrote it, but I'm over it. You two work your magic!"

Emily smiled shyly at Davey, wondering if he noticed that Shane had said they had *magic*.

Shane turned to the crew. "Okay, everyone, I want you to just let the cameras roll. We're probably going to do like twenty takes on this, so just get ready to be here for a while." Emily tried to hide her smile at the idea that she might be there with Davey all night. Shane took his seat in the director's chair, and hollered "*Action!*"

And they were off.

Davey began typing quietly at his computer while Emily worked in silence next to him. "I don't get how you're so good at writing html, Kelly," Davey said, after several long seconds of silence.

Emily was still looking at her screen, which was a long list of numbers and symbols. She was so focused that she almost believed she was writing a super-advanced computer program. "My dad always wanted a son, so he taught me what he thought boys should know."

"Okay, I get it, but—"

"The most important thing in code is clarity," Emily spoke in her character Kelly's know-it-all voice. She swiveled in her chair to face Davey. When their eyes

169

locked, Emily didn't notice the cameras silently filming her, or Shane's intense gaze, or the rows of empty desks. All she saw was Davey looking lovingly at her. Suddenly she wasn't acting anymore, she was looking at her true love.

"You really are something else," Davey said softly.

Emily didn't know what to say. Neither did Davey, evidently. They had already hit the main point of the scene, which was a moment of subtle connection between their characters. There was a long pause.

Suddenly Shane's voice boomed. "*And cut!*" He began clapping, slowly. Then he turned to the crew. "I think I speak for everyone when I say thank you for making that Hollywood's fastest take. Perfection!" Then, like a mental switch had been flipped, Shane said to no one in particular. "I'M GOING HOME NOW. GOODBYE, PEOPLE!" And then he stalked off the set.

Davey shook his head and laughed. He pushed his feet onto the floor and his rolling chair sailed backward on its wheels. Emily copied Davey's move and sailed backward in her chair so they were once again next to each other.

"That man is outta his mind!" Davey laughed.

Emily giggled, trying to connect with Davey without gossiping about Shane. Mac was crazy, but some of her rules had merit. "He *is* something else."

"You know, *you're* something else." Davey smiled at Emily. "You're a great actress."

Emily looked around the computer room to be sure he was talking to her. Spotting only the crew, she felt silly. *Of course he had been talking to her. She was the only actress on set.*

"Thanks." Emily shrugged. Her left leg was starting to tremble, so she stood up and pretended she needed to stretch. She locked her fingers behind her back to loosen her shoulders.

"And we really do work well together," Davey added. "I'm so glad we're friends."

Emily barely heard the part about friends, because her heart was in the process of dropping to her stomach. Davey Farris Woodward, A-list movie star, crush of her life, thought they worked well together? What else did he think?

Emily catapulted herself back to Earth. "So, what did you want to talk to me about before?"

Davey glanced around at the few crewmembers still lingering on set. "Maybe we could talk about it later, in private?"

"You should come to Mac's party tomorrow," Emily blurted out. She was pretty sure she didn't have the right to invite people, especially not Davey and especially since Mac was such a control freak about everything. But the words were out before she could stop them.

"I didn't know Mac was having a party. . . . " Davey sounded intrigued.

"Yeah," Emily offered. "To celebrate me and some

of our friends." Feeling extra confident from his earlier compliment, she tapped him once on the shoulder. "You can be my date." She said it like a joke because she wasn't brave enough to show she meant it. Yet.

"Hmmm. . . ." Davey pretended to think about it for a few seconds. Just enough time for Emily's heartbeat to race even faster.

"And maybe we can finally talk about that thing," Emily added leadingly.

Finally Davey grinned. "Sure. That'd be great."

"Perfect." Emily smiled. As of tomorrow night, she and Davey would be SkyWard.

chapter
TWENTY-TWO

mac

◀ Saturday   October 3 ▶

iPHONE OFF

t was 10:30 a.m. on Saturday morning, and even though Mac was wearing her softest American Apparel sweats, she felt like her skin was crawling. The worst feeling in the world to Mac was being out of control, and that morning there was so little she could control—starting with her party. In less than twelve hours, she would be hosting all of BAMS, plus half of Hollywood, plus paparazzi, plus caterers, at her Star Power party. More like *Star Powerless.*

Of all the days to be phoneless, today was the cruelest, Mac thought, as she sipped her acai berry smoothie, which their housekeeper, Berta, had made for her. Mac wasn't allowed to leave the house like a normal, civilized member of society, and she looked longingly at the Bel-Air canyons through her French windows. She felt like Rapunzel, stuck in her two-story Spanish villa, a prisoner in her own home.

Mac imagined sending a note by messenger pigeon to Elena to remind her that the dance floor needed to be big enough to hold at least fifty people. Would Elena remember? And more importantly, she wondered, how could she even get a pigeon without a phone to order it?

All her other notes were on her iPhone, which was confiscated until tomorrow morning, hours after the party *ended*. Mac still hadn't confirmed the playlist, or the sushi list, or the chocolate fountains (dark chocolate, not milk!), or the mocktails or the napkins (specially printed with pictures of the I.C.). Had she even sent that e-mail? Without her phone she had no record-keeping system. On top of *that*, Mac had no way to reach Becks to explain why she couldn't make her photo shoot, or to reach Coco to determine whether she had decided to change anything *else* about herself in the last several hours. There was only one solution to her technology meltdown—face time.

But *how* could she possibly get anywhere when Erin was off for the day? Public transportation was out, since the nearest bus stop was miles away. Besides, Mac wouldn't even know what bus to take. One false move and she could wind up in Pomona. She stared out the window where Jenner and his friend Ethan were practicing volleyball serves. Mac longed for their freedom. Ethan had a car and could leave any time he wanted to. . . .

And then Mac pressed mental rewind: *Ethan had a*

car and could leave any time he wanted to. But how could she convince him to drive her down to Venice? The situation seemed hopeless, but Mac knew that to give up then was to think like a normal girl. And Mac was *not* a normal girl. She bounded down to the backyard.

"Go away," Jenner said, the second he saw her. "You're grounded."

"Where are your manners, big bro?" Mac asked in a Splenda-sweet voice. "We have company."

"What'd you do, Mac L.A.?" Ethan asked. He was tall and gangly, with slightly bug eyes and a narrow face.

Mac didn't have time to get into the history of her situation. Her mother was downtown, visiting a client on the set of his new action movie. Her father was playing golf with Marty Scorsese in Newport Beach. So she had at least three hours until either parent returned. And if she couldn't convince Ethan to go to Venice, then she needed to start brainstorming a plan B.

"It's just a bummer." Mac sighed, ignoring Ethan's question. "Because all the Dixie Gals are waiting for me at the beach."

"The Dixie Gals?" Ethan stopped looking at Jenner and gripped the volleyball. "You mean like the surf models?"

"Mm-hmmm. We're like this." Mac crossed her fingers so it looked like they were tight. But actually she was crossing them because she was lying. "If we're ever in the same place, I should introduce you. . . ."

"But didn't you say you knew where they were?" Ethan asked. His eyes got even buggier.

"Well, Kip and Ella are in Venice," Mac said, making up names. *Why hadn't she learned their names?*

"Aren't their names Tully and Darby?" Ethan asked, looking confused. "And there's a third girl . . . from Hawaii? And for a little while there was a fourth?"

"Oh yeah," Mac said quickly. "*Kip* and *Ella* are my nicknames for them. And I call the Hawaiian girl Aloha. It's a really long, dumb story." Mac laughed, like it was just *too* funny. But she made a mental note to research Becks's teammates a little more. "My best friend is their new fourth."

"Don't feel like you have to be nice to her," Jenner called from across the net.

"Ethan and I are talking," Mac said, smiling fakely at her brother. "The Dixies are in Venice for a photo shoot before they go to the Maldives. If you want to meet them, today's actually a good day." Mac had no idea how she would introduce Ethan to girls who didn't even know her name, but she would worry about logistics later.

"Sounds like we should go today," Ethan offered.

"Dude, she's *grounded*," Jenner said.

"Jenner worries about everything!" Mac teased, hoping that reverse psychology might subdue her brother. Jenner opened his mouth like he was about to protest, but then he shrugged, probably remembering that he didn't actually care, and went back to his volleyball.

Mac looked at Ethan. "Look, I really can't stay long in Venice, but if you wanted to meet them I could swing it today."

Ethan glanced at Jenner, as if waiting for his permission, and then Mac. He took a deep breath. "Okay. I drive you to Venice. You introduce me to the Dixie Gals. Deal?"

"Deal." Mac smiled. It was almost too easy.

chapter
TWENTY-THREE

becks

◀ Saturday   October 3 ▶

10 AM   Arrive for Shoot in Venice Beach

8 PM   Mac's Star-whatever party

Becks trudged through Venice Beach, her Reef flip-flops sinking into the hot sand. Bulky men lifted weights on the boardwalk and joggers shuffled by in neon bikinis and orange-glow tans.

Becks adjusted her floral-print LeSportsac duffel bag over her left shoulder and headed toward a royal blue Dixie tarp where people were setting up lights and tripods. Her bag overflowed with everything she could possibly need—her black Dixie swimsuit, waterproof watches, and plenty of extra towels and sunscreen. Still, something was missing: Mac. *Not* Mac the agent—but the girl who could always make her feel better about anything. Ever since Xochi had dropped off the package yesterday, she'd felt like Mac was outsourcing their friendship to a professional.

Tully, Darby, and Lei were sitting cross-legged in the center of the Dixie tarp. Lei was French-braiding Darby's hair, while Darby ate a banana PowerBar. Tully was smothering sunscreen all over her freckled face. All the girls wore solid black Dixie bikinis, and Becks was relieved to match the group.

"Little sis!" Tully grinned when she spotted Becks. Her blond hair was in two French braids down the sides of her head. "Show us what you chose!"

Lei looked up from braiding Darby's hair and smiled brightly. "Yes! I need to know what color ribbons to use in your hair."

Clearly the other Dixie Gals had assumed choosing *authentic* accessories was a fun decision, like selecting what flavor milk shake to order from Sloopy's. And clearly being a stress bomb was not the way to win points with this group. Becks peered down into her duffel bag and stared at her options. She was afraid that whatever she chose would make her look like a tool but took a deep breath and pulled out her favorite bracelets. They were mahogany-colored wooden beads, about one inch thick in circumference. They were like the bracelets Mac always wore, but sportier. More importantly, they were *authentically* Becks.

"I'm going with these," Becks said fake-confidently, holding up the bracelets for the girls to see. "With these earrings." She pointed to the diamond studs already in her ears. They had belonged to her mother.

She waited for everyone to tease her.

"Niiiice," Tully said.

"That rocks!" Lei smiled warmly, and Darby nodded. "It's like . . . earthy glam!"

And that was it.

Becks felt a flood of pride: She had just made a style choice for herself. Why had she spent the past decade thinking she couldn't function unless she ran everything by Mac?

"Way cuter than what Tiana would have worn." Tully snorted.

Becks felt reassured every time she learned a little more about the mysterious Tiana. But before she could ask another question to be totally sure, Chad yelled to the group, interrupting her analysis.

"All righty, girls," Chad hollered. "Come meet your photographer, Blake." He pointed to a small skinny man who reminded Becks of a monkey because he was very short and had a lot of hair everywhere—on his neck, chin, and arms. Even his fingers were furry. He wore black pants and sipped from a ceramic espresso cup. "Hey there!" he called out warmly.

"Blake is the best surf photographer in the world," Chad explained.

"Oh, please." Blake seemed to wave away Chad's bragging. "Go on!"

"Girls, you ready?" Chad asked the DGs.

Becks expected more instructions to follow, but the Dixies leapt up. Blake swiveled across the sand, with an espresso cup in his left hand and a professional-looking camera in his right. Becks gulped, realizing they had run out of time to do her hair. She was the only one who didn't have French braids! The shoot hadn't even begun, and already she didn't match.

Becks followed the group to the sand and watched as Tully, Darby, and Lei leaned their arms on their boards, jutted their hips and smiled as though it were the most natural thing in the world.

"I love it!" Blake cooed. "The board is your best friend!"

Tully bear-hugged her board. "It's my BFF," she said. Darby and Lei giggled like they always did at Tully's antics. Becks laughed from the side as she observed her fun-loving friends.

Blake pointed at Becks with his espresso cup. "This one, too!" Becks had been hoping no one would notice that she wasn't actually modeling. That way there was nothing to mess up. Maybe she could sit this one out and jump in next time?

"Get in there, Becksy!" Chad called from Blake's side. He waved her on with his sandwich.

Becks walked over to the fourth board, which was already plopped in the sand. She pretended to lean on it like the Dixie Gals had done, but she felt very silly and awkward.

"Is she always like this?" Blake asked Chad, looking a little peeved, like Becks was refusing to work with *him*. Becks wondered if this was how Tiana had behaved.

"She's shy," Chad explained to Blake. "Show us some teeth, Becks!" Chad encouraged.

Becks mustered her facial muscles into the shape of a grin. She felt like a freak, realizing that everyone was hoping she would just *get on with it*.

"Aw, come on, Becks, smile like you're happy! Not like someone's pelting you with food!" Chad commanded.

"But maybe they should!" Blake called out ominously.

Then, much to everyone's surprise, Chad picked a tomato out of his sandwich and threw it at Becks.

She was so startled to feel a slimy vegetable land on her that she couldn't speak. Then she burst into giggles.

"Wonderful!" Blake said, circling Becks like a sand crab and snapping away. "Throw more food at her!"

"More!" the Dixie Girls cheered in unison.

"No! Don't!" Becks protested, lifting her arms to shield herself.

"I love this job!" Chad gleefully tossed another tomato at Becks. It landed on her left shoulder. "I get paid to chuck food at people!"

When it came to roughhousing, Becks's brain turned off and she just did whatever came to her. She picked up the sand-covered tomato and threw it back at Chad.

"Yes! That's it!" Blake cooed. "I love it!" He had climbed atop a ladder and was now clicking frenetically above Becks. "Look at me!" he commanded, pointing at himself.

Becks glanced up and saw bulbs flashing. So this was modeling? Having a food fight while a monkey man climbed ladders and cheered? Maybe modeling was like surfing—maybe she did better when she just focused on the next step and not the whole picture. She decided to only worry about having fun. Modeling would take care of itself.

"Suh-weet, Becksie!" yelled Chad.

"Beautiful!" Blake yelled.

The Dixie Gals laughed and ran over to Becks, who had unleashed her inner goofball. Blake put on a Bob Marley CD and Becks danced happily to the music like she was at an Inner Circle sleepover, doing moves that had nothing to do with the reggae beats. She pretended to walk like an Egyptian. She did the Twist. She waved her arms like she was grocery shopping, or like she was a human sprinkler. She did the Superman dance. Tully, Darby, and Dixie copied everything and Becks felt like she was finally worthy of their group.

Two hours passed. Finally, Chad clapped his hands. "Thank you, ladies, we are done."

"We rock!" Lei cried. The Dixie Gals hugged, and Tully pulled Becks into the huddle. "It was so much more fun with you!"

"Yaaaay, Becks!" the girls cried in unison.

"Hey Becks," Tully said as they untangled. "We're going to hang out at the pier tonight. You should come with us."

Becks paused for a second while she considered it. She *did* want to, but she had promised Mac she would attend the Star Power party. "I kind of promised my agent—I mean *friend*"—Becks corrected herself—"that I'd go to a party she's throwing. But I'd love to come some other time?"

"All righty," Tully sighed. "It's too bad, because afterward we're all crashing at Lei's and then going surfing in the morning." She shook her head fake-sadly.

"Next time," Becks promised, and then the Dixie Gals turned and headed up the beach.

And that's when Becks spotted a familiar silhouette approaching. That long blond hair. The bright white sweaterdress. The stacks of wooden bangles lining her arms. Mac was walking with her brother, Jenner, and a tall boy who Becks was pretty sure was Jenner's volleyball teammate. She watched curiously from the beach while Mac came toward her, leaving the boys to talk to the Dixie Gals.

Becks glanced down at her G-Shock watch: She was three hours late. She put her hands on her hips and waited alone on the sand beside Blake, who was packing up his camera equipment.

"Babe!" Mac reached out her arms for a hug. Reluctantly, Becks hugged her back.

When they untangled, Mac stopped and stared at Becks. "Um, B?" Mac giggled, eyeing Becks's black bikini. "What's going on with *this*?"

"What do you mean?" Becks tried to keep her voice steady.

"Um, hello? This was not in the instruction manual,"

Mac spoke in her joke-bossy tone, which somehow still managed to be far more bossy than jokey. "What happened to the suits I sent you?"

"You mean the ones I couldn't even get *wet*." Becks had to clench her teeth to stop herself from yelling. "And anyway, I needed *accessories*. We *had* to wear this suit."

"Babe, I'm your agent, right?" Mac replied. "You're supposed to trust me. Xochi's suits were cuter. But don't worry, maybe we can get a reshoot on the books."

Becks had passed the point of patience. She had listened to Mac for years, always wondering what she thought. She was sick of Mac only being in her life to tell her what to do—it used to feel like *guidance*, but now it was starting to feel like something else.

Becks looked at Mac, her lips pursed. "In case you forgot, you used to be more than my agent. You used to be my best friend."

"I still am!" Mac cried.

"Best friends show up," Becks said curtly. She crossed her arms while Mac stared at her, speechless.

"Okay, fine, you can hate me in the car, but we have a party to go to!" she said jokingly. She reached for Becks's hand, but Becks jerked away from her grip.

The Dixie Gals were ahead, walking across the sand to their sun yellow Mini Cooper, which as usual was parked in the closest spot to the beach.

"Last chance!" Tully hollered, dangling her car keys.

"One sec!" Becks screamed back.

"But what about the party? It's for *you*!" Mac cried.

But Becks had already started walking toward Tully, Darby, and Lei. She turned to Mac one last time. "Gotta go," Becks said. "I made plans with my *friends*."

To: Paige Harrington
From: Emily Mungler
Subject: T-minus 20!

The party's getting started outside, and I am
upstairs putting the finishing touches on my hair.
I am so nervous I can barely hold a flat iron. It's
really happening! Davey! Here! Us! Together!

AAH! I CAN'T WAIT!!!!

To: Emily Mungler
From: Paige Harrington
Subject: Re: T-minus 20!

Just breathe. And when SkyWard becomes official,
you better take a sneaky iPhone photo of the happy
couple and send it my way.

xxxxooooo
paige

chapter
TWENTY-FOUR

COCO

◀ Saturday   October 3 ▶

6:30 PM   Get ready for Mac's par-tay!

7:45 PM   Red-carpet arrival

C oco sashayed onto the long red carpet that led to Mac's Bel-Air house, looking very much like Cordelia Rose, a rock star in the making.

"Coco! Over here!" screamed a tuxedo-clad photographer.

Coco swiveled on her cowboy boots, lifted her red plastic sunglasses, and posed, one arm on her bell-bottom-clad hip, other arm dangling at her side. Pout. It was exactly how her mother always did it. Coco counted to three in her head to give them enough time to get a good shot. Then she took a deep breath, repositioned herself, and gave the photographers another set of shots.

Inside, Mac's Spanish-style house had been completely transformed into a twinkling sea of stars. Blue star-shaped lights hung from the ceiling and around the walls and even lined the floor, giving the room a soft blue glow.

Coco peered out the French doors for a full view of the party, which was mostly in Mac's outdoor living room. It seemed like all of BAMS had turned up. Coco spotted the Rubybots in matching green Juicy sundresses dancing with their arms above their heads. Over by the black marble fountain, the sketchbook girls were sitting with their hands in their laps, talking quietly. The guys from the water polo team milled around the barbecue. Coco smiled and headed toward the pool, which overlooked the canyon. Rumer Willis and Katherine McPhee were sitting on lounge chairs, laughing with Adrienne.

It wasn't just the guest list that was impressive—Mac had (predictably) gone all out. Coco stepped around a life-size cutout of herself dangling from the ceiling. It said CORDELIA ROSE in swirly white lettering. Another one of Emily was perched in the other corner. Mac had apparently custom designed life-size posters of the Inner Circle and ordered them just for the event.

Coco took a deep breath and stepped outside. When her foot hit the grass, the DJ lowered the music.

"Please give a warm welcome to Cordelia Rose!" he boomed. All of BAMS cheered wildly. Coco smiled and shrugged, slightly embarrassed, but loving the attention.

Just as Coco was about to find Mac, she felt an annoying triple tap on her shoulder. She turned.

Ruby Goldman. *Of course.*

"Heyhowareyou," Ruby said. It was not a question; it was more like a command to begin a conversation.

"Hey Rubes." Coco smiled coolly. "I'm good. Performing a lot these days," Coco added. There was no way she was going to let Ruby rain all over her VIP parade.

Ruby arched an eyebrow and snorted. "Oh, and I'm sure it has nuh-thing to do with who your mom is. . . ."

Coco blinked in shock: Usually parent-jabs were off-limits, but Ruby had gone from first gear to fifth in seconds. Coco quickly recovered from the diss—she'd certainly had enough practice with *that* recently. "For your information, Rubes, it has nothing to do with her."

"Mmmmmkay." Ruby smirked. "I can't wait to go online and buy tickets to the reunion tour." Ruby whipped out her BlackBerry. "Are they on sale already? I could buy them now."

Coco stared at Ruby, annoyed. *"Actually,* I'm not part of my mom's reunion tour. I'm performing my own songs. In *coffee houses."*

Ruby gasped like Coco had said *jailhouses.*

"It's indie, Ruby," Coco spat. "But I guess you're just a little too *mainstream* to get it," she added, with an eye roll.

Ruby's turquoise eyes twinkled while she digested what Coco had just said. "Um, kewl?" She ate a piece of lobster sushi.

Coco resisted the urge to cross her arms because she had read that it was a sign of defensiveness, and she did not want to appear defensive. "In case you didn't notice, I have my own new look," Coco added.

"I guess I figured the sequins were being dry-cleaned." Ruby shrugged. "And that you thought today was Dress Like a Cowgirl day."

"No, Ruby, it's part of my whole *persona*. In case you *also* haven't noticed, this party is kind of for me." She glanced pointedly at another life-size cutout of herself by the cupcake table. Ruby's eyes followed her gaze, and she read the poster.

"Ooh, Cordelia Rose, right! My bad! A fake name," Ruby retorted. "Way to keep it real."

Coco sailed on confidently. "I'd invite you to Java Joy for my next show, but I wouldn't want you to get jealous."

"Java Joy. That sounds classy. Gee, I'd love to come support. I'm sure it's awesome," Ruby hissed sarcastically. "Oh, one last question," Ruby asked.

Coco rolled her eyes. "Yes?"

"What does your *mom* think about all this?" Ruby smiled an evil grin.

"Why do you want to know that?" Coco stammered, taken off guard. Her mom didn't *know* about it, of course, but how could Ruby know that?

"Hmm . . . doesn't seem like this new *persona* would jibe with her new tour."

Coco paused for a beat. "My relationship with my mom is none of your business," she said finally.

Ruby's eyes slanted like a Siamese cat's. "Of course. . . ." she said mysteriously.

Coco set her shoulders back. No one was forcing her to be in this conversation, and she refused to be annoyed by the static that was Ruby Goldman for another second. Life was too short.

"Gotta go," she said, and stalked off. It was time to enjoy her party.

CHAPTER
TWENTY-FIVE

emily

◀ Saturday   October 3 ▶

7 PM   Do hair for Star Power party

7:45 PM   Red-carpet arrival

Even though there was a party outside, Emily refused to leave the Armstrong guest bathroom. She placed her hands on both sides of the marble sink and checked herself in the gold-trimmed mirror for the thousandth time. Davey Woodward would be here any second, and she couldn't take any chances.

She'd already spent hours flat-ironing, spritzing, and mussing her hair to make it look like she'd just woken up with it like this. She straightened the straps on her Agnès B. dress, borrowed from her film wardrobe just for the occasion, and wiped a bead of sweat off her face. Finally, she took a deep breath of the lavender mist that filled the bathroom and then stepped into the party.

Emily had made her way over to the Nobu sushi station, and was taking a tuna roll when Kimmie Tachman bounded over in a pink sundress. It might have been cute if she hadn't paired it with pink Converse and a pink polka-dot headband.

"Hey." Kimmie slid next to Emily with a concerned look on her face. She delicately placed a piece of sushi onto her plate. "Um . . . are you okay? Must be kinda rough, huh?"

Emily squinted. She had no idea what Kimmie was talking about. "Huh?"

Kimmie lowered her voice. "I heard all about your little, uh, secret."

Emily's mind quickly scrolled through a mental list of Things Kimmie Could Possibly Be Talking About, but she was stumped. And annoyed. The last thing she wanted was to be conversation-bulldozed by the Tawker when Davey walked in. What if he thought they were besties?

"Let's talk in private," she said quietly.

Emily reminded herself she had to be über-polite since Kimmie's dad was producing her movie—and because Kimmie had a way of blabbing if you got on her bad side. She followed Kimmie to a shady knoll on the grass away from the crowd, but vowed to get back to the party as soon as possible.

Emily crossed her thin arms. "What's up, Kimmie?"

Kimmie took a bite of her dragon roll. She pity-smiled and looked right at Emily, her brown eyes twinkling. "I think it's adorable that you have a massive crush on Davey and that he's the reason you came to L.A."

Emily's eyed widened. Thoughts bounced around in her head as she wondered a) how Kimmie could know,

b) what she wanted, and c) what she was going to do about it. Had Ruby put her up to this? Was Kimmie accusing Emily so that she'd confess? Had everyone on set come to this conclusion? Was it *that* obvious?

"My costar?" Emily laughed, as though the idea had never once occurred to her. She shook her head affectionately. "He's a great guy, but we're just friends."

"Don't worry, I won't live-blog about it or anything," Kimmie assured her.

Live blog? Emily's right leg started twitching. That was so not the kind of press she wanted. "Kimmie. I'm flattered that you care, but you've got it all wrong." She stared up the grass at the party, where kids were now dancing to a Taylor Swift song.

"Did Ruby put you up to this?" Emily asked suspiciously. Kimmie was nice, but easily swayed by the Rubybots.

"Look, I'm on Team Emily here." Kimmie tied the bow on her dress into a floppy knot. "But it seems to me that this could be a *great* story. You love him, you moved to be near him, and now you're working together. It would make such a great feature. A girl doing whatever it takes to go after her dream guy."

Emily exhaled with relief. Kimmie wasn't out for anything—she just wanted the scoop. Thank goodness she hadn't done anything naïve, like confess to the Tawker.

"Um, Kimmie? That's a really interesting story, but

it's just not true." She smiled sweetly, taking a step back toward the party. "Anyway, enjoy tonight!"

Kimmie raised one dark eyebrow at her. "Okay, Ems. But a word of advice." She paused meaningfully. "Watch your back."

Mac's Text Log

7:01 PM   Hey Becks, just saying hi and a reminder that the party starts now-ish.

7:02 PM   Hey Becks, 4got to remind U that the prty is at my house.

7:04 PM   Want me to send Erin to Malibu?

7:05 PM   FYI Erin says she would love 2 get U.

7:06 PM   U need me 2 look at outfit choices?

7:07 PM   B where R U?

7:08 PM   Becks U OK?

7:12 PM   Becks U there?

7:14 PM   B?????????????????????????????

CHaPTer
TWenTY-SIX

mac

◀ Saturday   October 3 ▶

8 PM   Partay partay partay!

Reminder: TAKE CHARGE!

Mac fluttered to the appetizer table in the foyer and took a bite of a mini quesadilla, holding it under her star-shaped napkin to be sure she didn't stain her favorite Vanessa Bruno dress (pewter, sleeveless, perfect). She surveyed her party suspiciously, making sure everything was A-list, but all Mac heard was the DJ's music and all she saw were people laughing and smiling. Her event was on the road to Hitsville, but there was no time to gloat. Already there was one huge problem: Becks *still* wasn't there.

Mac had already text-terrorized her friend, and she hoped the beach blowup was just a case of Becks being impulsive. Mac checked her front door for the tenth time in thirty seconds, wondering when Becks would breeze through. If she didn't arrive soon, she was going to miss the outdoor movie screening with highlight reels of Becks, Emily, and Coco and cameos by Clutch and Adrienne. (Much to her dismay, she'd had to *not* contact Cardammon out of respect for Co's privacy.)

"Hey," someone called from behind her. Mac turned around, her eyes searching the crowd, ready to wail on Becks for being so late, but hug her for being there at all. Instead, she saw someone she had *not* been expecting.

Davey Woodward.

At her party.

Uninvited.

Mac almost dropped her quesadilla in shock. How in the world could Davey have known about this? The invite list was very selective, and his name was abso-seriously not on it. He was the *last* person her brain wanted to see, even if her pounding heart suggested otherwise.

Davey was standing alone in the backyard look-ing around, his hands tucked into his Diesel jeans. He looked sweet and almost shy, which was especially cute for someone so famous. Around him, kids were trying to play it cool, even though he was a big deal, even for BAMS. The Rubybots smiled sweetly from the dance floor, and Hunter Crowe and the water polo guys tried to hide their curious glances. Everyone was checking him out, and clearly no one knew how to start a conver-sation with a movie star. It was almost funny to see her ordinarily fame-resistant peers made shy by a celebrity.

Mac looked at Davey and their eyes locked. For a second Mac wished they were all alone in her backyard under the stars, and that there wasn't a crowd of people around them. Her heart thumped and she had no idea how to snap back into control. *The only way forward is through,* she reminded herself of Mama Armstrong's life rule number twenty-three. Mac had to get through this.

She plastered a fake smile on her face and strolled down the grass. "Davey!" she squealed extra loudly, loud enough so that all her classmates could hear. "What are you doing here?"

"Mac?" he seemed surprised by her breeziness.

Mac herself was a little surprised at the acting skills she could summon in a pinch. She kept a perfectly fake smile on her face. She hugged him emphatically, holding the pose for an extra second or two, inhaling his Polo cologne. After she let go, Mac grabbed Davey by the pinky finger, and led him away from the crowd toward the willow tree that was further down the backyard.

When they were definitely out of earshot, Mac put her hands on her hips. "What are you doing here?" She couldn't believe she had to do this *again*. It was hard enough the first time. "I'm sorry you got the wrong idea, but I have already told you that *this*"—she pointed at herself and then at him—"can't happen." Even though she said it forcefully, a tiny part of her hoped that Davey would see through her act.

Davey put his hands on her shoulders and smiled knowingly. His hands fit perfectly around her shoulders. She felt dizzy as he pulled her closer. She leaned in and smelled his Polo cologne, mingled with a faint whiff of sweat. It smelled . . . *wonderful*.

She tilted her head up and looked into his steely blue eyes. Her lips began to quiver, and her heart pounded with excitement and terror. . . .

The part of Mac that was watching out for Emily told her to jerk back, but the part of her that wanted Davey overpowered her. "You have to stay away," Mac whispered, but even she didn't believe herself.

Mac's heartbeat quickened as Davey moved toward her. . . .

She could feel his breath near her cheek. . . .

She wasn't sure what to do next, except stand there. She felt paralyzed with excitement and butterflies.

And then Davey Woodward kissed her.

Mac knew that she should PULL AWAY RIGHT NOW, but her tingling nerves were making it impossible to move. She had no idea how you were supposed to kiss a regular person, let alone a colossal movie star, so she stayed there and let his lips touch hers for a nanosecond. It was just long enough to notice that they were warm and soft, and that, had they stayed like that a second longer, it might even have felt good.

But Mac's conscience forced herself to pull away. She looked at Davey nervously. He gazed at her, trying to study her reaction.

And then there was a gasp.

Mac whipped around. Emily. She was staring at Mac

and Davey, looking like she was about to throw up. The plate of mini cupcakes in her hands started wobbling.

Mac's heart broke for her friend, knowing that Emily had discovered the truth, in the worst way imaginable. Mac's problem had just gone from Code Red to Code Dead. And the party was only getting started.

emily

◀ Saturday   October 3 ▶

8:15 PM   Mac's par-tay!

E mily stared at Mac and Davey. Her heart was beating so hard she felt like she couldn't breathe.

Her mind scrolled through the events of the past few weeks. Suddenly it was all as obvious as the ending of a Disney movie. The tuna sandwich Mac had made "especially" for her before the kiss scene, the lectures about staying away from Davey, the Disneyland Invasion. . . . Of course! No wonder Mac was so desperate to "help" Emily. All that time, *Mac had been trying to steal Davey!*

"I can explain!" Mac cried, looking desperate. But as far as Emily was concerned, there was no explanation necessary.

Emily pointed her finger at Mac. Between gasps of air, she did her best to yell. "I NEVER—SHOULD HAVE—TRUSTED YOU!" She wiped her sweaty face with her forearm.

The party was insta-quiet. The DJ lowered the music,

people stopped dancing, and conversations came to a halt. All eyes were on Emily, who was too angry to realize she was giving one of the most thrilling, and most *real* performances of her life.

"Em, no, you don't understand—" Mac reached out her arms like she was going for a hug.

"TRAITOR!" Emily roared. She was so enraged that she didn't notice Coco's arm around her shoulders. Or that Davey was staring at her as though she'd flown in on a broomstick.

"I should go get some water." Davey gestured with his plastic glass and scampered away.

Then, realizing Davey was leaving *her*, Emily couldn't stand one more second of rejection. "I'M SICK OF ALL OF YOU!" she screamed. She jerked away from Coco's arms and burst through the crowd of BAMS kids, desperate to get as far away as possible.

"Watch where you're going!" a guy called as she accidentally bumped into him, spilling his purple drink all over his button-down. But she kept running and stomped back into the house and up to her bedroom, or rather, the stupid Gift Closet. She slammed the door so hard that the brass owl fell off the wall.

Emily plopped herself on the bed and tried to be calm. She closed her eyes and took three deep breaths. Then, like her mind had hit rewind and then play, she suddenly saw what a lunatic she had been, screaming at Mac and Davey in front of hundreds of people.

Humiliation and hurt mixed together in one blend of Terrible.

Emily reached for her computer on the glass night-stand, hoping to iChat Paige. She felt extra desperate, since she'd just alienated all her California friends. She glanced at her screen, but her BFF wasn't online. Where were friends when you needed them? Angrily, she slammed the computer shut and flung herself back onto the white Duxiana comforter, her cinnamon hair sprawling over the pillow.

She stared at the ceiling fan, which, like her mind, was spinning in fast circles. All of a sudden, her thoughts turned to Mac's words on her first day of shooting: "You're not in Hollywood unless you're stabbing some-one in the back or you're getting stabbed in the back."

So this was the real Hollywood. Emily Skylar had finally arrived.

CHAPTER
TWENTY-EIGHT

becks

◄ Sunday   October 4 ►

6 AM   Surf warm-ups

8:30 AM   First bell

B ecks and the Dixie Gals were lounging on a dark blue Becker blanket under the shade of the Dixie tent in Manhattan Beach. The tent was stocked with Crummy Brothers butterscotch oatmeal cookies and teriyaki mini rice cakes, and there was a rack of brand-new boards for them to try. Across the sand, Olympian Kerri Walsh was practicing her volleyball serve.

Becks felt a tiny pang of guilt for ditching Mac's party the night before, but she brushed away the thought as she dug her toes into the sand. Instead of going to the party, she'd had a great time with the Dixie Gals. They'd gotten ice cream sundaes on the pier and talked to the local surfer boys. Or, more accurately, Becks had watched while Tully, Darby, and Lei talked to the local surfer boys. Usually the boys talked to Lei first, because she was the friendliest, and then they got the courage to say something to Tully. And then, when they'd had enough, Darby usually announced something ridiculous, like that they all had to go to the bathroom *rightthatsecond*. And then they'd all move to another spot on the pier and start over with new boys.

Afterward, the girls spent the night at Tully's house and watched surfing documentaries. Becks still couldn't believe she'd found friends whose idea of a good night was watching four hours of real Pipeline footage.

Today they were passing time until Chad arrived to deliver their new custom-made Dixie surfboards, which were designed to fit the girls' exact heights and weights. The plan was to get the boards, do an early surf together, and then chow down on pancakes at Uncle Bill's Pancake House. Becks sighed happily: It was the perfect day.

Tully was flipping through the latest issue of *Surfer* and making fun of boys they knew from international surf festivals. Becks didn't personally know anyone they were talking about—she had yet to go to a surf festival as a pro—but she was happy to be quiet and listen.

Becks studied the tool in question. He had a shark tooth at the end of a leather rope around his neck. (Not cool.) But he was golden tan and his brown hair was sun-streaked (cool), no doubt from spending so much time in the ocean. He reminded Becks of Austin, who was hot. (Very cool.)

"I think he's kind of cute?" Becks said shyly. By now she wasn't afraid to express her opinions to the older girls, but she was always diplomatic.

"You think he's cute, huh?" Tully smiled mysteriously.

"Little Sis approves of Rio Vann!" Lei squealed with excitement and clapped her hands.

Tully rolled her eyes and quickly flipped to another page in the magazine.

"Rio looooves Tully sooooo much!" Darby said, smothering blue sunscreen all over her freckled nose.

"Tully hates every boy who likes her," Lei explained, as though Tully wasn't right there. "As you saw last night!"

"Rio's lame!" Tully cried defensively, but the way she said it, Becks didn't think she meant it.

"Hey dudettes," Chad Hutchins sauntered over, waving a stack of photos. "Who wants to see next season's campaign?"

"Me!" all the girls but Becks screamed in unison. Chad dangled the pictures high above their reach, while Tully swatted at his arm like it was a fruit tree.

"Let us see!" Darby commanded, holding his arm.

Becks stayed put on the blanket, deferring to the older girls. She just hoped she didn't look like an idiot. She winced, remembering all her silly poses. Had she really thrown a tomato at Chad? Had she really done those ridiculous dance moves?

"Okay, fine," Chad said, handing the stack to Tully. "I'll go grab your boards from the van. They're pretty sweet." He turned and headed back to the parking lot.

Tully grabbed the pictures, and, like a greedy squirrel with an acorn, darted back to the blanket and kneeled over them. The other girls huddled around her, clamoring for a peek. Tully began flipping through the photos like they were cards in a deck. "Nope. Nope. Nope again," she said. With every *nope* she slammed the picture facedown on the blanket. "Nope, nope, nope, nope."

"Chill out," Darby said, gingerly picking up a photo. Peering over her shoulder, Becks could see that it was a picture of the four girls, with Becks in the center. Becks was pretty sure it had been taken after the first tomato had hit her. She was surprised at how not-bad she looked. She was smiling confidently, leaning against her board. To her great surprise, she quite possibly looked . . . cute.

"Let me see," Lei whined, reaching for the photo from Darby.

Finally, Tully had gone through the entire stack. She sat up straight, her hands on her knees. "There is nothing to see," she announced. She shot an angry glare at Becks. "She's hogging every single shot." Darby and Lei stared at Becks like she had just slashed their surfboards.

Feeling their angry eyes rip through her, Becks gulped. "I'm sure there are some good ones of us all?" she asked hopefully.

Darby thrust the stack at her, and Becks looked at the

first one. It was *technically* of all the Dixie Gals, but Becks was in the center and the other girls were blurry, like they were part of the background instead of star surfers. Slowly, Becks flipped it over. The next one was just Becks, with her hands horizontal, doing the "Walk Like an Egyptian" dance. The next was just Becks, standing ankle-deep in the water. And on it went like that.

"It's like Tiana all over again," Tully muttered.

Becks felt a knot in her stomach. Suddenly, what had happened to the fourth Dixie Gal was no longer a mystery. "It's just one campaign," she said dismissively. It was true—it *was* just one campaign—the Dixie Gals were already in so many, and there would be at least four more in the next year.

Tully raised her eyebrows. "If it's *just* a campaign—"

"—then why do you bother?" Lei finished.

"No, I didn't mean it like *that*," Becks stammered.

"Do you believe she just said that?" Tully's face was stone cold.

"Is she insulting what we do?" Darby looked at Lei, who was scowling.

"We take this very seriously. This is our life," Lei snapped, in the meanest tone Becks had ever heard her use.

"I'm sorry!" Becks cried, but she wasn't quite sure why she was apologizing. What was wrong with being good at something? Becks felt her cheeks get hotter as she desperately tried to save herself. "N-n-no, what I meant was that there will be lots of other campaigns. You'll have lots of chances."

"Oh, look!" Darby snorted. "Now she feels sorry for us!"

"You know what?" Tully said abruptly. "I'm tired of talking about it." She smiled warmly. "Let's call it a day." Lei and Darby exchanged a knowing look.

"Oh, sure," Becks said, relieved this discussion was over. She hoped everyone was just tired from the sun. "Let's go."

"Ummm . . ." Tully looked at Becks like she smelled. "There's not really room in the car."

Becks's heart dropped. She knew the Mini Cooper hadn't magically shrunk overnight. Apparently there was room for her as long as she wasn't more successful than they were. "Oh, sure I can just call. . . ." Call who? *Erin?* Becks wasn't even sure if she remembered her cell number. Or if Erin could pick her up. But she would have said anything to end that awkward confrontation. "I'll be fine," Becks lied.

"Really wasn't worried about that," Tully snapped. The Dixie Gals fake-smiled, and they all started walking to the car.

"Okay, maybe next time?" Becks said meekly to their backs, even though she was pretty sure that next time would never happen.

CHAPTER
TWENTY-nine

coco

◀ Sunday   October 4 ▶

4:30 PM   Depart Bel-Air for North Hollywood

6:30 PM   Gig @ Java Joy

The artist formerly known as Coco Kingsley walked into the Java Joy coffee shop in North Hollywood, flanked by Mac and Erin. She scanned the crowd and saw lots of colorful sunglasses, knit caps, and vests, and she knew she had dressed just right. She'd worn big red plastic sunglasses, a tan leather vest with fringe, and the skinniest purple jeans she could fit into. Her dark hair was pulled back with feathery barrettes. (She still couldn't bring herself to cut it into a fauxhawk, as Erin had advised.) No one would know she was Cardammon's daughter here.

Despite her serene smile, Coco's heart was beating like she'd had a quadruple shot of espresso. After the disaster at the Star Power party last night, today felt more important than ever. Mac was a mess over the Emily situation, and Becks wasn't returning her calls either. Coco knew Mac could be difficult, but she also knew there must be more to the story. It felt like the I.C. was disintegrating, and there was nothing she could do about it. If tonight didn't go well, Coco had decided to call it quits on the whole indie songstress thing forever. Because if she tanked tonight, she couldn't blame it on her mother's fame. She could only blame it on her lack of talent.

Cordelia Rose was the third name called. Taking a deep breath, Coco walked to the tiny wooden stage in the middle of the shop and sat on a wooden stool under the warm lights. She balanced her guitar on her right knee and adjusted the microphone so it was about three inches from her face. She closed her eyes and felt the stillness of the crowd. Coco had grown to love that moment before a performance, when the audience was wondering if they would like the next act. She paused, waiting for someone to scream that she was Coco Kingsley, but there was only the hum of electricity.

And then, when she strummed her guitar, it was like she had entered a trance. Coco forgot about the crowds, and the do-or-die pressure, and what this meant for her career, and what the audience might think of her. She just focused on strumming her guitar. A simple, A-minor chord.

She sang three songs that night: first "Stay Away from My Latte," and then "Only I Can Knock My Fam," which were inspired by feeling so sad about Finn's diss. She finished with a cover of a Joni Mitchell song, and she stayed calm and soft without losing intensity. It was all over way too fast.

When she finished, there was a hush over the crowd. For three long seconds, she felt that stillness return, like they were at a surprise party and someone was about to yell. In the silence, Coco's mind had no focus and her worries returned full force. Were her songs too mainstream? Too intense? Coco gripped her guitar, bracing herself for the inevitable jeers.

Instead came applause.

It was slow at first, like a small trickle of water. Then, like a rainstorm, it grew to a crescendo, and Coco knew: She was a hit. She leaned into the microphone and whispered. "Thank you so much—I'm Cordelia Rose."

Smiling brightly, Coco looked out at the audience to get a better view of her new fans, who were *still* clapping. After all, these were the people she had to please. She had no idea how a hipster would bow, so she curtsied daintily. She spotted guys in skinny jeans and vests and plastic sunglasses nodding approvingly. As she stood up to get off the stage, she remembered her mother's advice about performing: "Always play to the back row." Coco looked to the far wall and waved to the row of hipsters sitting on the dilapidated yellow velvet couch.

And then she gasped.

Sitting there, in a body-hugging Hervé Léger dress, her face wrapped in a silk Hermès scarf, was Cardammon. Coco and her mother locked eyes for a millisecond, until Cardammon tilted her Gucci fedora over her face like a shield from the crowd. It was too late: She had already seen the devastated look on her mother's face.

The lie she'd told her mother about not wanting to perform washed over her like a shame-wave and Coco instantly regretted everything: standing there in public, using a fake name, and most of all, being caught by her mother in a lie. She felt like a fraud in her bohemian getup. Of course her mother was devastated: After all, Coco had lied to her, and then lied *about* her, pretending not to be her daughter.

She wanted to run to her mother and explain herself, but then she realized that the crowd was shouting for her.

"*Encore!*" a man yelled.

Soon the entire coffee house was chanting "Encore!" and Coco remembered she was still standing on a stage, in front of a full house of new fans. She imagined them throwing plastic sunglasses at her if she didn't perform another song.

The show must go on, Coco reminded herself. Heaving a shameful sigh, she sang a ballad she had written during one of her recent bouts of insomnia, "Don't Call Me Princess." It seemed ironically apt.

The crowd loved it from the first note—they cheered and held their cell phones high in the air, casting a blue glow across the room. As Coco strummed her guitar, she tried to let the music take over her mind, and to just focus on the lines:

No one really gets me
They all think they know
Who I am
But I'm no princess
And I ain't no brat
They don't know
Where I'm at
And they can't 'cause
I'm still figuring it out

Coco tried, but she just couldn't get into her song. Even though the audience listened quietly, she knew that her second set didn't have that magical stillness of her first. She couldn't wait to get off the stage and explain everything to her mom.

But when Coco finished and ran outside, she spotted her mother scurrying into her baby blue Bentley while her Brazilian, Swiss-trained butler held open the door.

Coco yelled to get his attention. "Pablo!"

He looked at Coco sadly as he closed the door. The car zoomed off.

Coco stood in the middle of the parking lot, the cold night air giving her goose bumps. Shivering, she ran back into the coffee shop bathroom, to warm up and hide. She was so distressed thinking about her mother that she didn't even notice that the audience was still cheering loudly for her, or that a man in a charcoal suit had shoved a business card into her hand, or that Mac had followed her into the bath-room.

"Congratulations, rock star!" Mac exclaimed proud-ly. She removed the business card from Coco's hand and Mac read it. "Apparently Adriano Lesher from Moon-shine Records on Sunset Boulevard wants you to call him." Mac paused to study Coco. "You know that's, like, huge, don't you, Cordelia Rose?"

Coco stopped splashing water on her face and looked at Mac. "My mom was here tonight."

"Oh . . ." Mac said. She didn't say anything for so long that Coco knew it was bad.

"I'll bet she was proud," Mac offered finally. "You nailed it."

"You should have seen the look on her face." Coco gripped the faucet to steady herself. She wished she'd never said anything to Ruby Goldman at Mac's party. Ruby had clearly set this up—there was no other way Cardammon could have found out about her gig, since she had used an alias. But more than anger at Ruby, she just felt disappointment in herself. Ruby hadn't made her use a fake name or lie to her mother. "Mum thinks I'm ashamed of her."

"But babe, you *were*," Mac said matter-of-factly. "You didn't want anything to do with her. I hate to say I told you so, but. . . ."

Coco's throat tightened. The last thing she wanted to hear was another reason why she was a bad daughter. "I thought this would make me happy," Coco said glumly.

"Music does make you happy," Mac said knowingly. "But it's hard to hide who you are in music. And part of who you are is the fact that you have a world-famous mother. So somehow, you're going to have to accept this."

Mac was right, but that didn't change what had just happened. As Coco tore the business card up and threw it away, her mind replayed the look on Cardammon's face again. And again. She just wished she could take it all back. It was going to take a miracle to prove to her mother how truly sorry she—*Coco Kingsley*—really was.

chapter
THIRTY

emily

◄ Sunday   October 4 ►

SORRY NOT IN THE MOOD TO UPDATE TODAY

E mily lay on her back on the white carpet, alone in the Gift Closet, watching the ceiling fan spin. She hadn't left the room since the party and she'd been subsisting on stale Chex Mix from her secret stash.

Earlier that day, Mac had knocked on the door and offered to take her to see Coco's gig at some coffee house, but Emily had pretended to be asleep. She was depressed, and homesick, and not ready to face Mac. It was easier to just watch the fan spin. In fact, Emily was *still* watching the fan spin when her phone buzzed. With great effort, Emily rolled onto her side and peered at the screen. It was an e-mail from Giselle, Shane's assistant. Emily hoped he hadn't decided, in their three-day break from shooting, to fire her. But if he had, then at least she could avoid D.F.W.

To: Emily Skylar
From: Giselle DeLaurentis
Subject: Final Scene

Message: Hey Emily. Good news! Shane had a meeting
with his spiritual advisor today and wanted you to know
that we'll be shooting the final scene (tomorrow). We're
re-setting it at a concert, and Miley Cyrus will be our
guest, performing on stage. Script revisions attached.
See you tomorrow! Best, G.L.

Emily looked at her phone, not sure what to make of
the Miley memo, so she decided to do what she'd always
done with important matters up until she moved to Bel-
Air: run it by Paige.

Emily studied her friend in the computer screen
window. Paige was wearing a denim jumper dotted
with red blobs (or were they hearts? Emily had no
idea), a yellow T-shirt, and a green scarf tied around
her head. Normally the getup might have made Emily
giggle, but she was too worried to laugh at that second. After they'd exchanged hellos, Emily poured
out the whole story of the party and the kiss and the
blowup. Just thinking about it made her head hurt,
and talking only made her feel worse. Now her stomach hurt, too.

"That was quite a party," Paige observed calmly.

Emily slapped her forehead. "I didn't even tell you

about the e-mail from Shane," she said, breathlessly. "I'm forwarding it to you now."

Paige's eyes darted across her screen. She didn't have an iPhone, so she had to read e-mails off her computer. "That's innnnnteresting," Paige said slowly.

"What if Miley is going to take my part?" Emily wailed. Nervously she tied the string on her Harajuku Lovers pajamas into a double knot just to do something with her shaky fingers. "Maybe they'll reshoot the whole movie with a new lead actress."

"You'll be fine," Paige soothed. She crunched on what appeared to be a Nutter Butter. "It sounds like he wants a cameo from a star. Directors do this all the time." Emily nodded, but even hearing it from Paige didn't make her feel much better.

"Ems? You okay?" Paige asked after a silence.

"No," Emily said sadly. "I wish I were in Iowa." She wished that her life was that simple again: that she could be sitting at Paige's house, eating Nutter Butters, and gossiping about stars' faux pas instead of making them. Why did she have to live in a world where she could only see her loved ones on iChat? Why had she chosen to live in a place where she couldn't trust anyone?

"But you know what? I will be!" Emily said suddenly. "I'm booking my ticket right now. I'm coming home where I belong." She opened a new browser window on her laptop, determined.

Paige shook her head. "Um, sorry, Em. I can't let you do that."

"What are you talking about? I'm coming home. I can't handle Hollywood." Emily found the first flight she could on Orbitz and took out her mom's in-case-of-emergency credit card. She typed in the numbers and held her hand over the keypad, ready to hit send.

"You *can* handle Hollywood," Paige's voice cut in, and Emily reluctantly switched back to the chat window. She watched as Paige retied her scarf-headband, her face dead serious. "You are forgetting who you are. These Hollywood peeps may have known you for a month, but I've known you for twelve and a half years. You are Emily Mungler, the girl who doesn't care what people think, which is why everyone thinks you're so cool. Screw Mac and her backstabbing. I miss you and I'd *kill* to have you in Iowa, but you need to stay there and see this out, for you. . . ." Paige's face was huge and bubble-like in the computer screen. She paused to breathe. "This is about you finishing what you started. This movie. It's about your dream."

Paige and Emily were quiet while Emily absorbed the monologue. For the first time in way too long, Emily's heart and mind were calm. It was amazing that no matter how far apart you were, a true friend could always make you feel better. Distance didn't mean a friend understood you less.

Emily closed the Orbitz window. "You're right," she said, a slow grin spreading across her face. "I *can* do this."

"Just don't go near tuna." Paige winked.

CHaPTeR
THIrTY-one

◄ Sunday   October 4 ►

5 PM Poolside chat with Mama Armstrong

Reminder: TAKE CHARGE!

Mac and her mother lay poolside at their house, basking in the hot Los Angeles sun. Adrienne wore an enormous wide-brimmed hat and sunglasses, an indication that she intended to stay outside for more than twenty minutes. Mac was grateful that her mom was willing to risk some UVAs today, because she really needed some time alone with her—not to mention a huge dose of A.L.A. wisdom. Mac felt terrible that Emily had seen her with Davey at her party. And that the micro kiss had happened at all. To make matters worse, Coco was seriously rattled from the whole Cardammon trauma, and Becks wouldn't return her phone calls.

"So I want to give you the heads-up that we may have a problem," Mac began in a confessional tone. She rubbed some Bain de Soleil on her legs so as to avoid eye contact.

"Go on," Adrienne said calmly, not looking up. She was making notes on a phone sheet.

"Emily's been in her room the whole day with the door locked." Mac sighed, staring out at the turquoise water. "I think she might want a new agent."

Adrienne put down her pen and looked up from her work. "I thought she was tired from the movie shoot."

Mac shook her head. She took a deep breath and began to explain the whole Davey/Emily disaster as quickly and as accurately as she could. While Mac spoke, her mother made tiny notes on her call sheet. Every so often she nodded her head so Mac knew she was listening.

"—and so now Emily thinks I've been trying to steal her FB—"

"What's an *FB*?" Adrienne squinted, trying to decipher Mac's slang.

"Future boyfriend," Mac explained.

Adrienne shook her head. "Honey, don't talk like that. It makes you sound not-so-smart."

"Fine." Mac took a deep breath. "And so now Emily thinks I've been trying to steal Davey, which of course is not true, but I'd think that in her shoes," Mac finished. Staring out at Maude's SpongeBob SquarePants raft, Mac couldn't help wishing there were life rafts for, well, *life*. Because right now she felt like she was drowning.

Adrienne lifted up her prescription Prada sunglasses and stared squarely at Mac. "Okay, so maybe Emily won't want to work with us anymore. It's not the end of the world."

Mac blinked in shock. "Is that all you're going to say? I might have just cost you a huge star. Aren't you mad?"

Adrienne shrugged. "Yes, Emily is going to be a big star, but it's always a risk that you'll lose clients. This is not an easy world, my darling daughter, and I see how you're giving this your all." Adrienne took her glasses off and smiled knowingly at her daughter. "And by the way, I think it's cute that you and Davey finally realized you liked each other."

Mac jerked back, like she'd been spritzed with Hillary Duff's With Love. "What do you mean, we 'liked each other'? *He* liked *me*!"

Adrienne crossed her legs and replaced her call sheet with that day's *Variety*. "Sometimes mothers know things, and I've known this one for a while. . . ." Adrienne sighed. "Then again, I'm exceptionally smart about human behavior."

Mac rolled her eyes affectionately. It was amazing how her mother seemed to know everything. As they said, information was power. No wonder her mother was one of the most powerful people in Hollywood.

"But sweetie, we'll have to talk about dating curfews," Adrienne continued. "I'm not even sure I want you dating until high school. Let alone an actor. . . ." She closed her eyes and shook her head. "Actors! Eek! They're the worst!"

"Mom!" Mac squealed. "We are *not* dating."

"Well, not yet, of course—you're too young," Adrienne mused. "But as your mother, my best defense is a good offense."

Mac smiled with relief as she eased back into her lounge chair. Of all the people she'd let down that week, at least her mother hadn't been one of them. But something was still bugging her. She sat back up. "What I want to know is, what could I have done? How could I have controlled this?"

Adrienne dropped her *Variety* and lay on her side, facing Mac. "You can't *control* people." Adrienne said *control* like it was a dirty word. "You can *steer* them, in what you think is the right direction. But at the end of the day, the only person you can control is yourself."

Mac nodded, thinking. Through her mind cycled all the times she'd tried to control her friend's destinies: yelling at Emily and Davey-blocking her, pretending it was about Em's career, when really she could have listened patiently, like a good friend, and tried *talking her* away from Davey rather than *forcing her* away from Davey. Managing Becks in a sport she knew nothing about, choosing outfits for her without listening to her concerns or taking the time to actually *check in* with her. Giving Coco an entirely new image, against her will. (Well, she stood by that decision.) But maybe she had taken it too far?

"You, my darling daughter, have a special situation here," Adrienne went on, shading her eyes to look at

Mac, "since these people aren't just your clients. They're your *friends*. It's not easy."

Mac felt like a load of guilt was lifted from her shoulders. If her own mother—whose life motto was *Make it happen*—was telling her the situation had been challenging, then it truly was. But she had an idea to make sure she never got so far off base again.

She took out her iPhone and erased the daily REMINDER: TAKE CHARGE. In its place she wrote, REMINDER: FRIEND FIRST, AGENT SECOND. Already she felt better.

Adrienne glanced down at her gold Baume & Mercier wristwatch, as if deciding how much more time she wanted to spend chatting. The answer apparently was no time at all. Adrienne abruptly stood up and wrapped her towel around her waist. "We need to move on," she said sternly, moving toward the house.

Yes, Mac thought. *We do need to move on.* And she already had a plan.

To: Emily Mungler
From: Paige Harrington
Subject: Good luck!

Just wanted to say one last time: Break a leg! (Well,
don't literally. Unless Shane wants you to play the
part as an invalid . . .) Anyway, as your mom would
say, this is your time to *be one* with the universe.
Can you feel the now?

Call me later. Remember: It's your time to shine.

xoxo
Paige

chapter
THIRTY-TWO

mac

◀ Monday   October 5 ▶

12 PM   Shoot on Location

2 PM   BIG SURPRISE!!!

Reminder: FRIENDS FIRST!

Mac stood in front of Staples Center on Monday afternoon, watching the cars whiz by. She looked very together in her J Brand jeans, Michael Stars tee, and a purple boho-chic scarf, but inside she was a wreck. They were shooting on location today at the famous stadium in downtown Los Angeles, and there was *still* no sign of Emily. Mac had carefully planned today out, and she wanted everything to go off without a hitch. She knew Emily was mad at her . . . and that she might never want to work with Mac again. But for Emily's sake, Mac hoped she wouldn't throw her own future out the window out of anger.

Mac was about to do something drastic when one of the union vans caught her eye. To her great relief, Emily leapt out.

Mac thought she might cry tears of joy as she watched Emily dart out of the van and follow the neon green arrows pointing the way to the shoot. She wanted to run over and tell her the latest news: Miley wasn't going to make it, and the producers had decided to use a hotter, fresher musician. But she knew she was the last person Emily wanted to see. Besides, the young starlet was already racing off to the set. Mac quietly followed behind, hoping that her top-secret plan might be salvaged after all.

Inside the Staples Center, it looked like everything was set up for a giant rock concert: There was a giant black stage in the middle with tons of lights hanging down. The seats were filled with teenagers. The only difference was that every single person in the seats was an extra, getting paid to be there. Mac felt jittery. If her plan didn't work, she'd be costing many people a lot of money.

She took her place in the VIP lounge behind the stage and the cameras, and watched the production assistants scanning the crowd, checking for overly tanned faces or Lakers logos. The scene was supposed to take place on the East Coast and anyone who looked "too L.A." was moved to the back rows, out of the camera range. Before she could worry about it another second, Mac spotted a young PA escorting Cardammon.

"Over here!" Mac yelled, waving her arms excitedly.

Spotting Mac, Cardammon sashayed over in a strapless dress and black suede heels that zigzagged up her skinny ankles. She slowly removed her oversize Chloé sunglasses. "Mackenzie, darling, please tell me why I'm here," she purred.

"It's a surprise, Cardammon," Mac smiled brightly. "But I promise it's a good one."

Becks arrived next, taking baby steps over to Mac. It was quite a peace offering for Becks to actually show up, since they hadn't talked since Becks blew off her party. (Or rather, since Mac blew off her photo shoot.)

"How've you been?" Becks smiled calmly at Mac. Her hands stayed put in the front pockets of her baby blue sweatshirt and she wouldn't make eye contact. She kept staring at the Staples Center floor.

Mac was so happy to see Becks that she hoped she didn't scare her away with affection. "Look, B, I'm so sorry about everything," Mac said in a rush, eyeing her friend hopefully. "I got a little—make that *very*—carried away. Please don't be mad at me."

"It's okay." Becks shrugged. "I'm not *mad* at you." She shifted her weight so she was standing on just her right leg. "I've just been . . . bummed."

Mac fidgeted with the ends of her silk Hermès scarf. "I stretched myself too thin." It was hard to admit that she'd screwed up, but it was the truth. "And I got too controlling. And, let's face it, I tried to be your agent the best I could, but maybe I just don't know enough about surfing."

Becks laughed, and tapped Mac on the shoulder affectionately. "Mac Little-A! I don't need you to know about that stuff." She tucked her strawberry blond hair behind her ears. "I just like knowing that you're there on the sand cheering for me. It's been kinda lonely without you."

Mac's heart soared. So her friend did miss her, after all. "I'm sorry. I'm still figuring out this whole being-an-agent thing, but I *have* figured out that my first priority is being a friend."

Becks turned red and each girl knew the other was truly sorry. Mac wrapped her arms around Becks, and Becks hugged her back.

Just then, Shane Reed stepped onto the stage clutching a loudspeaker. Turning to the thousands of extras, he boomed in a cheerful voice. "Please welcome Ryan Seacrest!" Mac had been so caught up in her reunion with Becks that she hadn't realized they were moments away from shooting the final scene. She crossed her fingers, and hoped for the best.

Mac, Cardammon, and Becks stayed seated in the VIP area behind Shane, who was peering into a giant monitor hooked up to the cameras. Mac and Becks looked at each other excitedly as the *American Idol* host stepped forward, in a navy suit with his hair perfectly in place, like a Ken doll.

"Next up," Ryan began in his trademark announcer-y voice, "we have the hottest new talent out of California. Please give it up for—"

A hush came over the crowd. Only the producers, Shane, and Mac knew who Ryan Seacrest was about to announce.

"—Coco Kingsley!"

The crowd applauded and the Inner Circle roared. Mac peered over at Cardammon, who was covering her mouth with her long French-manicured fingernails. She seemed too shocked to move.

Behind Cardammon, Mac spotted a scraggly figure whom she hadn't seen in days: Finn Grace. She'd invited him to come check out Coco, knowing that if she could make a believer out of *him*, she could make a believer out of anyone. Besides, she knew how dementedly obsessed Coco had been with getting his approval. But she hadn't expected him to show up. He caught her eye and coolly tilted his pageboy cap in a gesture of hello. Mac nodded back, just as coolly.

Coco strutted onstage, looking once again like her old self, in a Topshop minidress and Moschino ankle boots, and even a sequined vest. Mac knew Coco had realized there was a reason for sparkle onstage—it really popped. Coco smiled and waved happily to the stadium. If she was nervous, it didn't show. She seemed completely at ease in her slightly pop, very eclectic, very *Coco* getup.

Sitting on bleachers in the back, Kimmie Tachman's mouth dropped. Mac smiled proudly, knowing she and her live blog—not to mention Ruby Goldman—would see just how far Coco had come.

"Thank you, everyone. My name is Coco Kingsley," she purred demurely into the microphone, Cardammon-style. "And this one's for my mother."

Cardammon gasped and Mac beamed as her friend took the stage and tilted the mic toward her.

For the next five minutes, Coco sang a rocking acoustic version of Cardammon's hit single "Forever Blue." She seemed just as relaxed and happy as she had that first day back at Karma. And the crowd was as calm and appreciative as the café crowd had been. They, too, were quiet from the first note to the last. When Coco finished her song, the stadium erupted in thunderous applause. Coco smiled to the group and curtsied daintily, her mother's signature sign-off.

Mac looked over at Cardammon. A tear trickled down Cardammon's Mystic-tanned face. She angled her head to face Mac and mouthed the words, *Thank you.* Mac simply nodded.

Just then she felt a tap on her shoulder. She turned around to find Finn Grace, his pageboy cap in hand and his dark hair askew. He wore a red tee that said EMPIRE RECORDS. "Your friend was amazing up there. I mean, she just *owned* it," he said, an excited gleam in his eye, like he was coming down from a music-induced high. "I just wanted to say thanks for inviting me. And, um"—Finn shuffled nervously from foot to foot—"I was wondering, do you think Coco would mind if I told her that? I kind of said some things the first time we met and I didn't know if she'd want to see me again. . . ." he trailed off.

Mac raised an eyebrow. She had seen boys in crush

mode before, but it was always amusing to watch a hipster admit he actually cared about something. "I think she'd like that."

Finn smiled gratefully, and his whole face lit up. He'd actually be kind of cute, Mac thought with an appraising eye, if you cleaned him up. Her mind shifted into makeover mode: definitely a haircut (Gianni?), a little bit of a tan (natural, not Mystic), and of course a full-on wardrobe overhaul (Xochi now styled men)— until she reminded herself that she had enough projects on her hands.

As Finn thanked her and made his way toward the stage, Mac smiled and twirled the Inner Circle ring she wore at the end of her long gold chain. As much as she wanted to be an amazingly talented agent, she had learned one thing in the past month: None of it mattered if you didn't have your friends. Sure, it was a big moment for Coco and Emily's careers, but it was an even bigger moment for them all as friends. Mac raised her iPhone and took a picture, so she could remember it forever.

CHAPTER
THIRTY-THREE

emily

◄ Monday   October 5 ►

2 PM   Call time = Time for my A-game

Emily's heart beat rapidly as she watched Coco finish a spectacular performance. Coco had been totally fearless, like she was singing in front of just the Inner Circle—and Emily hoped she could do the same. She was seconds away from re-shooting the kissing scene, and her heart was pounding with nervous energy.

In the script, she and Davey were supposed to get caught smooching by the stadium camera, which would broadcast their kiss on huge screens above their heads, just like at a basketball game. Emily gulped. If she failed, there would literally be thousands of witnesses. She took the last Wintergreen Altoid from the box and chewed anxiously.

Emily glanced over at her costar. Davey wore an ankle-length flowery dress that looked like it had been borrowed from the wardrobe of *Kit Kittredge: An American Girl*. It had a floppy white lace collar and covered his arms all the way down to his wrists. And yet, even in a *ridiculous* getup, Davey Farris Woodward *still* looked adorable. She chuckled to herself. Most girls in America would do anything to kiss Davey, and here she was getting paid to do it. And she had been *thisclose* to giving it all up.

"Last looks!" Shane boomed. It was time for their close-up.

Tina dabbed bronzer on Emily's face, and Robyn ran a comb through her hair.

Soon the crew swooped around her and Davey, and the boom mic was in position. Davey turned to Emily and smiled warmly. "Break a leg," he said. Even though they'd sat side by side for Coco's performance, they had not actually said a word to each other since Mac's party.

"Thanks." Emily nodded, grateful for the effort. As their eyes locked, she tried to read his facial expression, but it was neutral. Was he wishing he was kissing Mac? Was he thinking what a lunatic she had been at the party? Emily clenched her fists, stopping herself. This wasn't about Davey. It was about getting to live her dreams. It was about making herself proud. Instead of thinking about all the things that could go wrong with her very-public kiss, Emily remembered all the reasons why she wanted it to go right. She didn't move from Iowa and leave her best friend and mom behind just to spend her time thinking about a boy. She'd moved to

L.A. to be a movie star. Emily summoned her courage, and inched closer to her costar. *Everybody loves confidence,* she reminded herself.

Shane removed his fedora to wipe his head with a handkerchief. Without his hat, his head was shaped like a giant egg. "You ready?" he called through his megaphone.

Emily nodded confidently.

"And, *action!*" Shane barked through the loudspeaker.

Davey snapped into his character mode and faced Emily. "Look, Kelly, there's something I need to tell you—" he began.

Emily put her index finger on his lips to shush him. "It's okay, Tiff . . . Or should I say, *Tom.* I already know."

"How did you know?" Davey-as-Tom stammered.

"That day on the rugby field." Emily smiled in character, but for once, the real Emily was having a great time.

"Oh man, I'm so sorry—" Davey put his hands on his face as if to hide.

And seeing him so cute and vulnerable in a dress, Emily surprised even herself: She threw her hands on his square shoulders and gave him a soft kiss, right on the mouth.

Once their lips touched, Emily wasn't sure what else to do. The only thing she knew about kissing was that you were supposed to keep your eyes closed. She'd practiced in her bedroom on a pillow, but Egyptian cotton hadn't prepared her for this moment. She just pressed her lips against his in a very PG-rated, very minty-fresh moment. It wasn't fun or gross; it was warm and soft. In the back of her mind, she hoped Mac saw and was a tiny bit jealous.

Seconds later, Emily pulled back and opened her eyes.

"Wow," Davey said, his head tilted in surprise. "I didn't see that coming."

Of course he hadn't. In the script *he* was supposed to kiss *her*. Emily shrugged. "I like you," she said truthfully. She meant it as her character Kelly *and* as Emily. And then, realizing she'd just kissed a boy in a flowing dress in front of thousands of strangers, Emily felt a wave of giddiness wash over her. She tried not to laugh, but suddenly all the tension of the past two weeks made her erupt in laughter. And she couldn't stop. "You're wearing a dress!"

Davey glanced down at his outfit and soon he couldn't stop laughing, either.

They giggled for several seconds before Shane finally yelled, "CUT!" Shane leapt off the stage and ran toward the two stars.

Emily expected Shane to whip off his fedora and tear his hair out. She had gone completely off script, kissing Davey instead of letting him kiss her, she'd added lines that weren't there, and she still couldn't stop giggling.

To her surprise, Shane threw an arm around her shoulder. "Wham-o! You nailed it, Iowa!" Emily beamed. She'd just wanted to get through the scene, but this praise was icing on the cake. Especially considering how badly she'd screwed up the last time.

Smiling hugely, Emily spotted Chris, standing shyly by the crew. When their eyes met, he slowly clapped his hands together. Emily waved him over.

When Chris was close, she turned to Shane. "You have to meet my friend Chris Miller. He's been a star P.A., and he's saved my life so many times."

Shane looked at Chris as though he had never seen the boy in his life. "Well, Chris, we have to be sure to get you a good job on my next movie."

Chris puffed out his chest and extended his long skinny forearm to Shane. "That would be rad, sir!"

Shane turned to Giselle. "Make a note to hook up our friend Chris next time, OK?" Giselle nodded and typed something into her BlackBerry.

Emily and Chris shared a big smile right as Coco and Becks bounded over to hug her.

"You rocked!" Coco squealed. She was still dressed in her sparkly getup from her performance, her face aglow.

"That was huuuuge!" Becks cried, throwing her arms around Emily to wrap her up in a big hug.

Emily grinned, grateful they were there to support her. She took a step back from Becks's arms and studied the crowd, which was filtering out of the stadium. Emily spotted Kimmie waving at her, and she waved back enthusiastically. She spotted Elliot Tachman and Cardammon, and then, out of the corner of her eye, she saw Mac walking toward her, shyly. Mac seemed concerned, like she had something to say. Becks and Coco shared an uncomfortable glance, and took a few steps back so Emily and Mac could be alone.

Mac took a deep breath. "I'm really sorry I kissed Davey. I was kind of crushing on him, and I got carried away. But I honestly never set out to do that." She toyed with the gold chain around her neck and stared at the floor.

Emily nodded. She knew Mac was telling the truth. And yet a million questions swirled through her head: Had Mac always liked Davey, or did she only want him because Emily wanted him? If Emily hadn't caught them at the party, would they have kept kissing? And could she really be Mac's friend again, and live in Mac's house, knowing that Mac and Davey liked each other?

"I'll never talk to him again, if you want," Mac added, her blue eyes serious. "If I had to choose between you and Davey, I'd pick you in a heartbeat. Every time."

Again, Emily knew Mac was telling the truth. And the fact that she'd never see Davey again . . . it didn't totally make up for the lying. But it was a start.

Emily glanced over at Davey, who was talking to

Shane, his dimpled face looking more adorable than ever. She thought back to all the hours of her life she'd spent dreaming about Davey Farris Woodward. All the posters on her wall back at home, all the time logged on his fan club website, all the late-night conversations with Paige about what it would be like to be his girlfriend. It had been fun, and it had meant something to her then. But now she realized: it didn't matter. Sure, it was a wonderful crush—in her head—but she didn't even *know* him. She hadn't known him then, and even after working with him, even after *kissing* him, she didn't really know him now.

The realization shot through her like she'd just chugged one of Mac's Red Bulls and Emily took a deep breath. Suddenly, she felt free. From her childhood crush, and from all the craziness that had come with it, ever since she set foot in Hollywood. She didn't regret her Davey-mania—after all, it was what had led her to that premiere party in the first place. Her crush had started this all, and it had brought her to Mac. But it had served its purpose, and now it was in the past.

"It's okay," Emily said finally. "You don't have to do that. I'm over Davey." As soon as the words escaped her lips, she knew she meant them.

"You are?" Mac asked tentatively. The worried yet hopeful look on her face said it all: she thought it was too good to be true.

"Yup," Emily said, more confidently this time. "And

I'm not mad that you liked him. I just wish you'd told me. But I'm willing to give you another chance." Of course Mac wasn't perfect—she just needed to admit that a little more often.

Mac beamed, relieved. "So does this mean I can still be your agent?"

"Yeah," Emily nodded, a smile slinking across her face, "as long as I can still be your friend."

Becks and Coco tiptoed back. "Looks like the Inner Circle is back on track." Coco grinned, putting an arm around Mac and Emily.

"Good cause I hate not seeing your updates on my phone!" Becks cried, waving her iPhone joyfully in the air.

"Ladies," Mac said, snapping back into alpha-mode. "Not only are we back, but this is only the beginning."

Emily smiled. She thought about how far she had come since Mac's pop quiz on her first day. Although Mac was usually right, sometimes she wasn't: You didn't know you belonged in Hollywood when someone was stabbing you in the back.

You knew you belonged in Hollywood when your best friends were right there with you.

acknowledgments

Thanks to the talented trifecta: Joelle Hobeika, Sara Shandler, and Josh Bank. It's been a great ride! I'd also like to thank Ben Schrank, Lexa Hillyer, and Jessica Rothenberg for their wonderful guidance. I'm grateful to Kristin Marang and Andrea C. Uva for their style savvy. Special thanks to Joanna Schochet for reading this many times beyond the call of friendship, Colleen Shaw for her impeccable taste and funny, Abby Stern for her exquisite LA eye, and Ruby Boyd for her smart insights about life and junior high. I'm very grateful to Tracey Nyberg and Jacqueline Regts for their production expertise; and Rachel K. Scott and Stephanie Jacobs for being neighbors extraordinaire. Thanks to Larry Decker for his encouragement and camera angles. And last but not least, thanks to my English teachers, who taught me I could write: Sharon Jones, Joe Kelly, and Gregory Rhodes.

Can't get enough TALENT?

Visit
ZoeyDeansTalent.com

The place to be for
downloads,
giveaways,
the TALENT blog
and more!